IN SEARCH OF MURDER

IN SEARCH OF MURDER

An Inspector Alvarez Mystery

Roderic Jeffries

This first world edition published 2013
in Great Britain and 2014 in the USA by
SEVERN HOUSE PUBLISHERS LTD of
19 Cedar Road, Sutton, Surrey, England, SM2 5DA.

British Library Cataloguing in Publication Data

Jeffries, Roderic, 1926–author.
  In search of murder. – (An Inspector Alvarez mystery; 37)
  1. Alvarez, Enrique (Fictitious character)–Fiction.
  2. Police–Spain–Majorca–Fiction. 3. Murder–
  Investigation–Fiction. 4. Detective and mystery stories.
  I. Title II. Series
  823.9'14-dc23

ISBN-13: 978-07278-8353-7

All Severn House titles are printed on acid-free paper.

Severn House Publishers support The Forest Stewardship Council™ [FSC™],
the leading international forest certification organisation. All our titles that
are printed on FSC certified paper carry the FSC logo.

MIX
Paper from
responsible sources
FSC
www.fsc.org   FSC® C013056

Typeset by Palimpsest Book Production Ltd.,
Falkirk, Stirlingshire, Scotland.
Printed and bound in Great Britain by
TJ International, Padstow, Cornwall.

ONE

Louisa looked across the pedestrianized road at a woman on the beach who had just stood to rearrange the towel on which she was sunbathing. 'There's Myrtle. Rather silly of her to wear a mini.'

Serena said, 'Who's that with her?'

'Her cousin.'

'Just for his stay?'

'That's what she says and he does have the same tired look. He's officially at the Bay Hotel.'

'They say that's become rather downmarket.'

'Out here, what hasn't?'

Louisa regarded her empty glass. 'Just for once, shall we have another?'

'Why not?'

She signalled a waiter, who did not immediately respond. 'They're getting ever slower.'

'They're islanders.'

The waiter walked a zigzag between tables and chairs. Louisa stood as he reached them. 'I'm losing the shade. You can move my chair.' She was convinced she spoke good Castilian.

'Certainly, señora,' he answered in English. He picked up her chair and moved it under the full shade of the sun umbrella secured through the centre of the table.

Louisa sat. 'Two gins and tonics and make certain it's Gordon's and not some kind of home brew from Menorca.'

'Two Gordon's gin.' He picked up the empty glasses, placed them on his tray, returned into the bar.

'Did I tell you I met Neil the other day?' Louisa asked.

'Which one?'

'Picare. George introduced me.'

'I thought you'd met Neil before?'

'George didn't know that so he was his usual pushy self.'

'The ex-pats' shaker and mover.'

'He likes helping people.'

'And the drinks they feel bound to offer in return. Was Neil in one of his more pleasant moods?'

'Very pleased-to-meet-you mode.'

The waiter returned, placed glasses on the table, spiked the bill, hurried to answer a call from another table.

'He invited us to pre-lunch drinks,' Louisa continued.

'Was the wife around?'

'George isn't married.'

'Of course he isn't. Was Neil's wife there?'

'Back in England for a week.'

'That explains . . .'

'What?'

'It's probably someone trying to be nasty.'

'So much more interesting than someone trying to be nice. Whose marriage vows is he hoping to help break this time?'

'Jane Calvert's.'

'Very unlikely. She lacks the courage to take the risk of Eustace finding out.'

'So, what did you think of the house?'

'Wonderful situation and with all that glass, it's like living in a view. But God only knows what the air-conditioning costs.'

'He won't worry about that. So, you've yet to meet the wife . . .'

'Well, tell me, what's she like?' Louisa asked.

'I wouldn't want to sound snobbish . . .'

'Overcome the bourgeois reluctance.'

'It's not difficult to think they're right and she did serve behind the bar before they married. By the way, did he say they're going to give a get-to-know-you party.'

'The only people who'll bother to go will be the usual crowd who cannot forego free food and drink. He did ask George where he should buy the champagne.'

'Why, when one can get cava everywhere? I suppose they'll be out to make an impression and serve Non Plus Ultra.'

'Not cava, Champagne; Krug.'

'I was forgetting that the pleasures of the common man

are not for them. Have you any idea where all his money came from?'

'No, because, surprisingly, he didn't talk about it. But there were paintings of Suffolk and Clydesdale horses on a wall in the study. Maybe he had something to do with farming.'

'Farmers don't make his kind of money.'

'Then he just liked the heavy breeds.'

'He married Cecily.'

TWO

Alvarez was awakened by the telephone; it took him a moment to accept he was in the office. As he used the arms of the chair to draw himself upright, the ringing ceased. He relaxed, closed his eyes. Something ignored should be forgotten.

The phone rang again. He swore, reached out and lifted the receiver. 'Tell me.'

'Is that Inspector Alvarez?'

He was tempted to deny the fact.

'Policia Umbert here, Puerto Llueso.'

Any local policia should have known better than to ring him early in the afternoon. When he looked at his watch, he was surprised to find it was late afternoon.

'Inspector, I am reporting the death of Señor Picare who lived in Vista Bonita.'

'Normal or accidental death is the policia's concern.'

'After the doctor had examined the dead man, he said I was to suggest you came here as soon as possible.'

'Why?'

'He said nothing more to me or Rosalía.'

'Who's she?'

'The cook.'

'Who else is there?'

The señora and Marta who works in the house and the cleaner Carolina.'

'Is the señora hysterical?' Hysterical women made a man helpless.

'She's in bed.'

'Has she been given a sedative?'

'Dr Ferrer said—'

'Ferrer?'

'Yes.'

Alvarez had visited the medical centre a short time before

because he had judged himself to be suffering from something. Ferrer had examined him. 'Your complaint is your lifestyle. Stop smoking, exercise a lot more, eat a lot less and restrict your drinking to half a glass of red wine and a tin of lager each day.' Why hadn't he suggested an alternative cure: suicide?

'Are you still there, inspector?' Umbert asked.

'Who found the body?'

'Rosalía. Managed to get him out of the pool, but when the doctor arrived, he pronounced the señor dead.'

'Was it a heart attack, a stroke?'

'The doctor said he drowned.'

'How?'

'In the swimming pool.'

'I'll be there as soon as I can.'

'The doctor said you should come immediately.'

'He can wait.'

He studied a plan of Urbanization Reus and located Vista Bonita on the top road which ran along the flank of Puig Grege.

He left the office, walked along to the old square and Club Llueso. Roca, the barman, moved along the bar. 'Don't often see you at this time of the day. Not able to enjoy your siesta?'

'A coñac without comment.'

'You lead a rough life.'

'Cheer me up me up by telling me more things I know.'

'When you're miserable, you like to make everyone else feel miserable.' Roca moved away. Alvarez brought out a pack of cigarettes, tapped one loose, lit it.

Roca returned with a filled glass. 'Has someone tried to blow up the government and failed to make you so cheerful?'

'A doctor.'

'And said you're fit enough to continue working?'

'I'm waiting for the verdict.'

Roca looked uneasy. 'I . . . I hope I've not been speaking out of tune?'

'How could I yet know?' Alvarez drank.

'Here, you're not . . .? Is the trouble serious?'

'So far, no one can tell.'

'I'm damned sorry, Enrique.'

'Forget it.'

Roca picked up Alvarez's glass, refilled it. 'At a time like this, one needs help.'

Alvarez turned off the main road and on to the side one which led to Puig Menor, at the foot of which were several houses and bungalows. Originally, there had been several requests for permission to build on the crest of the high hill, or low mountain, but these had been denied until the weight of the brown envelope matched expectation.

The road had not looked particularly steep, but it was poorly fenced and to a man who suffered from altophobia, it was dangerous; a slight mistake and the car might veer over the side, turn over and over, land with such force that it burst into flames. Care and luck enabled him to reach the top without disaster. Vista Bonita was large and in appearance typically Mallorquin – many different roof levels which provided a cheerful, higgledy-piggledy outline.

He parked alongside a red-and-yellow painted policia car, knocked on the panelled front door, rang the bell. The door was opened by a young woman and beyond her he had a shortened view of a hall, sharply illuminated by the sunlight coming through the ceiling lantern. Air-conditioning kept the area cool.

He introduced himself, since it seemed she would say nothing, asked her name.

'Marta Espinar,' she responded without looking at him.

Her dark brown eyes showed she had recently been crying; her long, jet-black hair framed an oval face which possessed no great beauty other than that of youth. She spoke so quietly he had to concentrate to understand what she said. 'Do you know where Policia Umbert is, Marta?'

She nodded.

He waited, but she said no more. The young met death less frequently than had their parents; she seemed confused by it. 'I want to have a word with him so will you show me where he is?'

She crossed the hall, passing through the broad shaft of sunlight, and at the end of a wide corridor stopped to open a door. He thanked her, entered a sitting room, insufficiently spacious to be the main one. For the staff, he judged.

He spoke to the seated man in uniform. 'Policia Umbert?'

'That's me.'

'Inspector Alvarez.' He went forward and shook hands. A member of the cuerpo was senior and superior to a policia, but it helped co-operation not to make that too obvious.

'Dr Ferrer still here?'

'He had to leave because of an emergency.'

'Did he discuss the señor's death and why he wanted me here?'

'Not really.'

'Let's sit and you can tell me as much as you learned.'

They sat, Umbert drew in a deep breath as if about to deliver a speech. 'The cook found him under the water in the swimming pool. She pulled him out and the doctor was called, but the señor was dead.'

'And the señora?'

'Seems she collapsed when she was told.'

'Did the doctor sedate her?'

'Don't know, but I wouldn't think so.'

'Why not?'

'Rosalía told him that the señora had been drinking heavily. You'll know that booze and sedatives don't like each other. Seems odd she should drink when her husband's just been hauled out of the pool.'

Umbert had not yet had to face the death of a close relative or friend. When Juana-María had died, he had left the hospital, returned to Llueso, and drunk himself insentient. The pain had not been lessened, merely temporarily lessened. 'Will you find Rosalía and tell her I want to talk to her.'

He watched Umbert hurry out of the room. When young, one rushed through life, squandering the energy one would nostalgically remember when older.

There was a 'free' Spanish newspaper in English on one of the small individual tables. Alvarez picked it up. Some pages listed advertisements and, as well as houses for sale and renting at foreigners' prices, there were details of adult relaxation. He was surprised by the frankness with which young ladies promoted themselves.

There was a knock on the door and he closed the newspaper, replaced it on the table; better not to be thought to be interested in some subjects.

Rosalía entered. 'You want to talk to me?'

'Please sit.' He studied her as she walked over to a chair. Seemingly calm despite what had happened. In shape, nicely moulded; in looks, unremarkable except for her mouth whose lips were generously inclined to voluptuousness. Not a head-turner, but very capable of attracting a man's interest. 'Thank you for coming along,' he said as she sat. 'I need to ask you a few questions and hope they will not disturb you. I understand you are the cook?'

'And a good one!'

Was there a cook who did not believe she was five star? 'Are you preparing the meal for tonight?' The question had surprised her, deliberately so. Subdued shock could be kept at bay by casual conversation.

'The señora must eat.'

'What will you cook for her?'

'Since he is tragically no longer with us, *Pollo al ajillo.*'

A favourite of his, joints of chicken seasoned with salt, lard, oil, and many teeth of garlic.

'That can even make a vegan hungry.'

'And cooked by me, he would eat it.'

'But from the way you spoke, the señor didn't like it?'

'Garlic made the breath smell. As if that should limit what one eats.'

'He can't have been interested in food.'

'His favourite dish was sausages and mash.'

'You cooked that?'

'He paid my wages. If he lacked taste, it was not for me to educate him except when he told me to call him Don Picare, not Señor Picare.'

'You did so?'

'Of course not. Spending much money did not turn him into a hidalgo.'

'He was very rich?'

'How else would he have lived here and paid me the wage I asked?'

He returned to more germane facts. 'I understand you were in the kitchen before you tragically found him in the pool. Tell me what caused you to go out to the pool?'

'The phone rang. Señor Russell wanted to speak to the señor. The señora had gone out, so I guessed the señor was in the pool and went out with the cordless phone. He was all floppy at the bottom of the pool.'

'You called the police?'

'I stripped off and got into the water to try to save him.'

'You are a strong swimmer?'

'No.'

'Then it was brave of you.'

'It was something I had to do.'

'What happened in the pool?'

'I dived under and got hold of him, managed to drag him to the steps at the shallow end and lift him up so his head was above water. I shouted for Marta, told her to call the policia, then help me. She wanted to have hysterics, but I made her assist me drag him out of the pool. When the policia arrived, they tried giving CPR, but it was too late.'

'Was the doctor here quickly?'

'Quickly enough, but he said it wouldn't have been any good if he'd flown.'

'Nothing more?'

'What more is there to say?'

'The doctor wants to talk to me. When that happens it usually means there's a problem and he's worried about something. D'you know where's the body?'

'Taken to the morgue.'

'I gather the señora is in bed. Have you spoken to her since the tragedy?'

'She came back from her day out shortly after I found the senor, I told her what happened and I've kept an eye on her ever since. She's sleeping.'

'Thanks, apparently, to drinking well.'

'What if she did?'

'For her, that was kind.'

'Do you have any more questions?'

'I'm afraid so.'

'Then would you like some coffee and biscuits before you ask them?'

Her aggressive manner had softened. From experience, he knew that tragedy could create a temporary emotional bond. 'I certainly would.'

Seated in the kitchen, he watched her pour beans into the coffee machine which had so many controls it probably needed a sharp mind to master its operations. She opened one of the higher wall cupboards and brought out a plastic container, then two plates from a lower cupboard which she put on the table. 'I think you'll like the shortbread since you've the look of a man who knows what to enjoy in life.'

He had eaten shortbread before. He helped himself to a second oblong piece; that was followed by a third one at her encouragement.

The coffee flowed into two cups. She put a sugar bowl and small, elegant red glass jug with cream in it on the table. 'What d'you want me to tell you?' she asked as, seated, she added sugar and cream to her coffee.

'You mentioned Señor Russell. Have you met him?'

'Frequently.'

'He often comes here?'

'Yes.'

'A good friend?'

'Of the señor.'

'But not of the señora?'

'He seldom came if she was here.'

'What do you think is her objection to him?'

'He drinks heavily when he does not have to pay the bill.'

'That is not unusual.'

'One cannot honour fine food if one's taste is dulled by alcohol.'

'He didn't care what he ate?'

'I cooked *Perdiz a la Montañesa* and he tasted nothing.'

However much Russell had drunk, it seemed inconceivable he had not appreciated quartered partridge fried in oil until golden brown, served with a sauce of onion, paprika, parsley, oil, salt, and lemon juice. 'If he didn't enjoy that culinary triumph, he must have been seeing treble, not double.'

'He would not have known had it been dried cod.'

'For him, a wasted banquet.'

'And when they began arguing, a noisy one.'

'What was their problem?'

'How would I know? You think I left the door open in order to hear?'

'Of course not.'

'However . . .' She paused. 'Perhaps it was female trouble.'

'A conflict of interests since the señor is said to have enjoyed many lady friends?'

'It is not for me to malign him.'

'It is your duty to tell me.'

'Do you have a daughter?'

'I am not married.'

'Then if you have one, you will have left the poor mother to protect her.'

'Now you're maligning me. Protect her from what?'

'Her own stupidity.'

'We're going round and round in square circles. What are you trying to tell me?'

'A naive young woman will dream when a rich man smiles at her.'

'Who is the young woman?'

'Marta.'

'And the man was Señor Picare?'

She did not answer.

Alvarez walked into the medical centre in Llueso. There were many people waiting in the square around which were the consulting rooms of several doctors. As he walked towards the one in which Dr Ferrer practised, a woman came out and another got up from one of the chairs and walked forward.

He hurried to check her. 'Wait a moment. I have to speak to Dr Ferrer.'

'I am next,' she said belligerently.

'Cuerpo.'

'We are now a democracy and even the likes of you takes his turn.'

'I am not ill and—'

'You are here to buy fish?'

'It is a matter of great importance and I will be as brief as possible.' To prevent further objection, he hurried into the interview room.

Dr Ferrer briefly looked up, then back down at his desk. 'Pascual Serra?'

'No, I—'

'Martin Rossello?'

'I'm here to—'

'You have not registered. If your visit is not in the nature of an emergency, you will first do so and then take your turn.'

I'm Inspector Alvarez of the Cuerpo.'

Ferrer visually examined him. 'Have I not relatively recently examined you?'

'Not exactly. We met—'

'You have put on weight, having undoubtedly ignored my advice. Get on the scales.'

'I don't need to be weighed.'

'Do I inform you what to do in your work?'

'I'm here in connection with the death of Señor Picare. He drowned in his swimming pool.'

'Having been called to his house, I am aware of that fact.'

'Because he drowned . . .?'

'You know more than I do until the post mortem?'

'He might have died from some other cause?'

'Unlike you, I cannot yet answer.'

'I imagined—'

'An unfortunate habit in both your occupation and mine. Why do you want to speak to me?'

'I'm not certain—'

'Another undesirable trait.'

'Is it possible the señor did not die from downing?'

'There are facts which need to be considered. There was no fine froth about nose and mouth. On the flesh above his right knee was a cut. I examined his nails and they were too well trimmed to have caused such injury while he struggled, as all drowning persons do; there was nothing about his swimming trunks capable of inflicting such a cut.'

'You think, then, that death was probably not accidental?'

14

14 Roderic Jeffries

'A possibility which has to be considered.'

If Picare had not died accidentally, there would have to be an investigation likely to be long and arduous.

'I imagine you are ill-acquainted with international crime,' Ferrer said.

Local crime was more than enough.

'You will be unaware that one of the more successful methods of murder in England at the beginning of the last century was initially considered to have been a case of accidental drowning. The murderer, who married several times in order to gain the small capital each woman owned, in turn disposed of each "wife" to gain her money. He provided a small tin bath in which to wash and, when she was lying in it, he put a hand under her head, an arm under her raised knees – the bath was that small – and as quickly as possible pushed down on her head and pulled up on her knees. As is now well known, the sudden impact of water on the back of the pharynx or larynx causes vagal inhibition and sudden death.'

'You're suggesting someone suddenly grabbed the señor and pulled his head under the water to kill him?'

'I am not.'

'But . . .?'

'I am naming a possibility. The lack of fine froth is indicative, no more. The slight bruising on an ankle might have been caused by a very minor bump; and as I have said, there was nothing in the pool or on his trunks to have caused the cut.'

'How is one to know for certain what happened?'

'The post mortem may provide the answer.'

'And if it doesn't?'

'Then it will be for you to decide.'

'But without a definite medical opinion, that may be very difficult, even impossible.'

'My patients are being forced to wait, so you can leave.'

Dolores, Alvarez's cousin, looked through the bead curtain which hung between kitchen and sitting/dining room. 'Supper will soon be ready so there is no need to drink any more.' She withdrew.

Jaime, her husband, waited to make certain she was not

standing behind the curtain, watching, and slowly, to avoid the noise of running liquid, refilled his glass.

'I've had an emotional morning,' Alvarez remarked.

'She said "no"?'

'There's a young woman, an older girl, really, who works in a large house. The English señor, a womaniser, was after her and filled her head with dreams of marrying him after he'd divorced his wife and living a life of luxury. A try-on which very seldom fails; one more reason why it's nice to be rich.'

Dolores stepped through the bead curtain, flicked away a trail which had caught on her shoulder. 'Can I believe what I have just heard?'

Puzzled, they stared at her.

'What have you heard?' Jaime finally asked.

'That were I unable to manage any longer on my own with the unending task of keeping the house clean, cooking meals for which no wife need apologise, seeing the children are sufficiently tidy to go to school and I employed a young woman to help me, I must expect that one of you, perhaps both, would claim imaginary wealth in order to dishonour her?'

'That's absurd!'

'You did not say "it's a try-on which seldom fails; one more reason to be rich"?'

'Enrique said that, not me.'

'And did you contradict a statement so contemptuous of women's purity or did you remain silent because you agreed?' She returned into the kitchen.

'Trust you to upset her when she's preparing supper,' Jaime said bitterly, in a low voice. 'Now, she won't take half the trouble over cooking she should.'

'She didn't understand what I meant. Judging the kind of man Picare obviously was, it was to be expected.'

'He's after them all?'

'Why not when he had money?'

'Some people are born lucky.'

'His luck ran out. He drowned.'

The phone rang. They waited for Dolores to answer the call. There was a shout from the kitchen and Jaime reluctantly went through to the entrada to pick up the telephone. The phone call reminded Alvarez he had intended to speak to Salas on his return to the office; it would do for tomorrow.

Jaime returned, carried on through to the kitchen. 'Aguenda wants a word.'

Dolores had been concentrating on the contents of a saucepan on a low heat. 'Take this.' She handed him a wooden spoon. 'Keep stirring, but not fiercely or you'll have everything bubbling out on to the stove.'

He watched her leave. Aguenda was more interested in other people's affairs than most and the chat with Dolores could continue a long time, leaving him stirring. Years before, no Mallorquin male would have been asked to help with the cooking.

THREE

Alvarez opened the bottom drawer of his desk and brought out a glass and half bottle of Napoleon Peteca, poured himself a generous tot. The brandy was rough, but one did not buy a Bisquit Dubouche merely to gain confidence.

When the glass was emptied, he lifted the receiver, dialled. 'Yes?'

Ángela Torres, as did Salas, spoke to someone as if from on high. For her, Salas could do no wrong. Had she been younger and of a less pugnacious nature, one might have wondered if her feelings for Salas were more than professional. 'Inspector Alvarez from Llueso.'

'What is it?'

'I need to speak to the superior chief.'

'He is exceedingly busy.'

'This is important.'

There was a silence before Salas said, 'Yes?'

'Inspector Alvarez, señor, from Llueso.'

'I am aware of that.'

'I have been investigating the death of Señor Picare.'

'I am also aware he drowned in the sea.'

'In his swimming pool, señor.'

'Then your previous report was inaccurate.'

'Señor, I did not say the sea.'

'Was he English?'

'I think so.'

'It has not occurred to you to determine so necessary a piece of information? Where is his pool?'

'By the side of his house.'

'I was asking where the property is located.'

'Above Urbanization Reus. That's on the south side of the main road from Llueso to Mestara. The doctor seemed to suggest the drowning was not an accident.'

'What does "seemed to suggest" mean?'

'Dr Ferrer mentioned some facts which he would not have expected. There had not been a fine froth about the nose or mouth, there was a cut on one leg which could not have been caused by his fingernails, because they were very well-trimmed, swimming trunks, or anything about the pool; there was slight bruising on one ankle.'

'In the face of those facts, why is Dr Ferrer not more certain? Have you misunderstood him?'

'No, señor.'

'Then you will speak to him again and ask for a firm opinion.'

'He mentioned a case in England which he thought might be relevant.'

'What was the case?'

'A man more than once married a woman with some money and each time he drowned her by suggesting she washed in a tin bath—'

'It is hardly credible to quote a case from the Middle Ages.'

'I gathered this occurred towards the end of the nineteenth century.'

'A time at which no bathroom in Spain was without running water and a proper bath.'

'But on this island . . .'

'Bears no relevance to circumstances on the Peninsula. There, after the first murder, signs of the struggle would have been efficiently noted and the man found guilty, suffered the penalty of death and no further woman would have suffered.'

'It seems not, señor. By pushing her head under the water with one hand and pulling up her legs with the other, an un-expected rush of water hits the larynx . . . or the pharynx . . .?'

'You are not aware where each is situated?'

'Not exactly.'

'Or inexactly. The larynx is a cavity in the throat which encloses the vocal chords; the pharynx forms the cavity which is the upper part of the gullet. Is that what caused Picare's death?'

'Dr Ferrer said there could be no certainty until the post mortem and even then there might not be any.'

'A typical medical excuse for failure. When will the PM be?'

'I don't yet know.'

'What is it your intention to do before that takes place?'

'It's difficult to know what can be done until we know the result.'

'A typical excuse for doing nothing. It is not necessary to learn the señor's financial situation, who were his friends and acquaintances, was he known to have caused deep resentment, had he been the subject of threats?'

'Is there any point in doing all that before the cause of death is established? If it becomes clear that death was accidental, all the work would be wasted.'

'Was the dead man wealthy?'

'I should imagine very much so.'

'I prefer fact to the product of your imagination.'

'In order to provide a base for his house, it must have taken many hours of work with heavy machinery to level the land . . .'

'You may omit technical details with which you are unlikely to be cognisant. If wealthy, that provides a motive for his murder.'

'But as yet, señor, there is no certainty . . .'

'You fail to understand that an hour's investigation taken immediately after an incident is worth far more than one undertaken later.'

'But in this instance—'

'You will question the doctor and demand a firm judgement, not possibles and perhapses. You will question the widow and staff in order to appreciate all the relevant circumstances surrounding his death. Is that clear?' Salas did not wait for an answer, cut the connection.

Alvarez awoke and discovered his siesta had lasted only slightly more than an hour. Salas had disturbed his sleep pattern. The rising heat from the marble window ledge, wavered and had a hypnotic effect; he closed his eyes. He had made his report and Salas could hardly expect him to carry out a futile investigation immediately.

Dolores' call from downstairs awoke him.

'Enrique, are you dead?'

'Did she expect him to answer if he were? He reluctantly got up, went through to the bathroom and enjoyed a cold shower, dressed. In the kitchen, Dolores was seated at the table, reading. He waited for her to put the book down, prepare his hot chocolate and set out biscuits on a plate. She continued to read. He coughed, then again.

'You have a cold?'

'I have to return to the station.'

'Since you are already very late, no doubt you will wish to do so quickly.'

'I thought perhaps you could make me some chocolate?'

'Will you still be awake by the time it is made?'

He would quickly acknowledge she was generous with affection and kindness, to others as well as the family, but her tongue could be sharp.

She closed the book, stood. 'It was ready when you were due to come downstairs. Since it seemed you were not working any more today, I drank it. Do you expect me to prepare some more for you?'

'It would be very kind.'

'As my mother used to say, expectation costs only words.'

He sat, looked across the table at the cover of her paperback. It was at an angle and he could only read the words: *Love is . . .* Did it finish off *Eternal Happiness* or perhaps *The Devil's Sword*?

'What are you thinking?' she asked as she lit a gas ring, turned it down to low.

'How deceitful life can be for a young woman.'

'You have discovered a conscience?'

'She's nothing to do with me. Marta works in a rich, married man's house. He chases women and recently filled her head with thoughts of his divorcing to her benefit.'

'She has not yet gained a true understanding of men and does not realise what he desires and how little he will pay for it. How do you know about her misfortune?'

'One of the other staff told me he is always on the prowl, especially after other men's wives, yet now he is taking an interest in her.'

'He is English.'

'Why d'you think that?'

'I have read that their behaviour will surprise even a Dutchman.'

'You read it where?'

'In a magazine.'

'A saucy one from the sound of it.'

'You think I would pick up such a monstrosity, let alone read it?'

'Then I have to wonder how . . .'

'You have told her how stupid her hopes are?'

'She would neither believe nor take any notice of what I said.'

'You see no reason to overcome her disbelief? How typical of a man. Find reason not to do something until it is too late to attempt it.'

'The danger is over for her. The señor has drowned.'

'Occasionally, there are times when there is reason to believe justice is not only for the few.'

'There's the possibility his death was not accidental.'

She went over to the cooker and began to prepare the hot chocolate he wanted.

'The superior chief has ordered me to start an investigation even though there is no certainty there is any reason to conduct one.'

'A Madrileño sees a rainbow when there is neither sun nor rain.'

FOUR

Alvarez rang the bell, waited, rang it again.

Rosalía opened the door. 'I can't fly downstairs.' She pulled the door more fully open for him to enter. 'What d'you want this time?'

'To have a word with the señora, if that is possible?'

'It isn't.'

'She is too distressed?'

'Naturally.'

'Is Marta here?'

'I decided she needed time at home.'

'Did she really believe the señor would divorce the señora and, after a decent interval, marry her?'

'At her age, wishes may still come true.'

'I remember, when I was a nipper, thinking I'd be a millionaire, own a great farm, breed the finest animals and grow the sweetest fruit.'

'And you've ended up pushing your nose into other peoples' lives.'

'And their deaths. I want a word with you.'

'You are not doing so now?'

He smiled.

'Would you like some coffee?'

'That would be great.'

She showed him into the large sitting room, not the staff one. He wondered why, forgot the question, went over to the picture windows, stared at the bay below and the surrounding mountains. Confirmation that nature could offer a no more beautiful scene.

He sat. The room was furnished for effect and comfort; the large fireplace, in which a wood burning stove had been unnecessarily placed since there were four radiators, had a carved marble fire surround; a couple of paintings hung on one wall, their subjects sufficiently indistinguishable to be great modern art; on another wall was a large, framed photograph of an old binder, dawn by two heavy horses, collecting up the cut corn and discarding it in sheaves.

Rosalía returned with a silver salver on which were two cups of coffee, sugar bowl, milk jug, and a plateful of almond biscuits. They ate, drank, chatted and it was half an hour before he said, 'Tell me about the señor and señora.'

'What is there to tell?'

He stood, produced a pack of cigarettes and offered it.

'We are not allowed to smoke in the house because the smell disturbs the señora.'

He started to return the pack to his pocket.

'That does not mean we do not smoke in the house, just that we do it somewhere where she is unlikely to go.'

She accepted a cigarette, he lit a match for both of them, returned to a chair. 'She is very susceptible to cigarette smoke?'

'Maybe. Or perhaps it had unfortunate memories for her.'

'Why unfortunate?'

'Ask her, not me.'

'Would you say she's a pleasant person?'

'As long as nothing goes wrong.'

'And the señor?'

'He had very little regard for anyone but himself. Like all men, he wanted to be thought more important than he was and as I may have told you, demanded we called him Don not Señor Picare.'

'And you rightly refused. Did he often irritate you like that?'

'Never more so that when he said my *Pollo al ajilla* tasted peculiar when it was good enough to serve at a royal banquet.'

'The English regard garlic with deep suspicion because it drives the devil away. But I'm sure you never made your annoyance obvious.'

'Not even when he often saw me for the first time in the morning and nipped my bum.'

'You didn't complain loudly?'

'It was always just a friendly nip.'

'I believe he liked to drink?'

'As much as anyone, more than most.'

'Did he enjoy many friendships?'

'If that is how you wish to describe the company of the women.'

'Were they mostly single or married?'

'Various.'

'You weren't worried by all that?'

'Am I fifteen years' old?'

'Did it disturb Marta?'

'Probably, but she never said anything.'

'But didn't it make her think that if her daydream came true, it would sooner or later for her turn into a nightmare?'

'She is old enough to understand that after marriage, a man continues to enjoy himself at the expense of other women, whether vizcondesa or peasant.'

'Didn't the señora raise strong objection to what went on?'

'He entertained his women when she was not here, but with friends; no doubt the women amused him when their husbands were away. In any case, she is not the kind of person to complain, not even when he went to England for a couple of weeks or more, leaving her here on her own.'

'She was very lonely?'

'That is not for me to say, but I did what I could to cheer her up.'

'Why did he return to England when he had such fun here?'

'Maybe he entered a retreat in order to punish his flesh.'

'You think that's possible?'

'I believe in little green men from Mars.'

'Did you ever talk to him, find out about his life, like how he became rich? Did he win a lottery?'

'Not really, except one day, I prepared a meal for him and the woman he'd brought back – the señora was away, of course. Perhaps the woman was acting like a puta, but she had more manners than him and later told me how much she enjoyed my wonderful cooking.

'He'd drunk a great deal and after she'd left in a taxi, he made it obvious he wanted me to join him with another bottle. I did not want to, but as he paid my wages . . .'

'The mule heeds the harness.'

'You think of me as a mule?'

'A gazelle. Did he appreciate your kindness?'

'Not after I'd shown him he'd be on his own until the señora returned.'

'Did you ever learn about his life before he came here?'

'He owned a farm and sold the land to a firm who wanted to build houses and was ready to pay a great deal of money for it. That he had become wealthy encouraged the señora and she married him and left the bar in which she'd been working.'

'How do you know all that?'

'I can't remember.'

'You must do.'

'Then tell me what I remember.'

'Try harder.'

'Someone must have told me . . . Perhaps it was the woman who came out on holiday and we met in the chemist when I helped her get what she wanted. He came in, saw her and hastily left. She spoke simple Spanish and started talking about him over coffee at a café. They'd been together until he got tired of her. She wanted to get her own back by saying that in England he had been no more than a peasant. I could have told her that.'

'What else did she tell you?'

'She met him somehow, some sort of agricultural show, I think. Described him as the horniest man she'd ever met. The señora kept him at arm's length until he was suddenly rich. Then she shortened the lead until he gave in and married her.'

'Money solves many problems. It's getting late, so I must move.'

'I think it is not so late you will refuse another coffee, this time with a little coñac.' She stood, picked up the cups, carried them over to the coffee machine.

His thoughts wandered. Picare had enjoyed affairs with married women which immediately aroused the possibility of a vengeful husband. But if every husband who was given a pair of horns immediately and invariably murdered his wife's lover, or lovers, there would be a shortage of men.

She placed cups and two small glasses of coñac on the table, sat.

'How did you get on with the señor?' he asked as he stirred sugar into his coffee.

'As well as can be expected.'

'You will stay here?'

'If the señora wishes. She enjoys good food and does not ask for sausages and mash.'

'He did?'

'I have said.'

'Will Marta remain?'

'The señora will probably ask her to.'

'How would you think the other English regarded the señor?'

'As if I could know. But if they thought of truth, not his money, they would say he was born to a very different life from the one he tried to live.'

'When will the cleaner, Carolina, be here?'

'She had to go to the dentist, but should soon arrive. I suppose you want to ask her a thousand questions. Will you wait? It is easy to make some more coffee and there's still coñac in the bottle.'

Being young enough to have avoided the oily, fatty diet necessary before the island had known prosperity, Carolina had a slim figure and the self-confidence which that brought. She sat opposite Alvarez in the staff sitting room. As attractive as Rosaliá, was his judgment, but of a different character; she was calm, cool and collected, Rosalía was a rocket with a touch paper waiting to be lit.

'Tell me about the señor and señora,' he said, after he had greeted her and explained why he wanted to speak to her.

'What is there to tell?' For a Mallorquin, she spoke quietly.

'For instance, was it pleasant to work for them?'

'Would you ever call it pleasant to work for someone who pays you?'

'Difficult to answer, but certainly I would know when it's unpleasant. Were they friendly to you?'

'So long as I did not forget they were employing me and therefore, in their view, a lesser person.'

'Would you say they were happy together?'

'After they had been married for many years?'

'Did they ever argue, have rows?'

'Neither of them was a saint.'

'I've been told that on one occasion, not long before the señor died, they did have a very ugly row.'

She was silent.

'You knew nothing about that even though it was during the day when you would have been working in the house?'

'What happened was their business not mine.'

'Nor was it mine until he died suddenly. Now I have to try to understand the reason for that row.'

'I can't answer.'

'Do you think someone might have killed him rather than that he died accidentally?'

'I don't know. Why would I think like that?'

'I have to ask again, did you often hear them arguing fiercely?'

'He had a quick temper.'

'On that particular occasion, their argument was so fierce it might easily have ended violently. Did it?'

'Impossible to answer.'

'Why?'

'I cannot say whether the worst row I heard is the one you're talking about.'

'It's over and done with. How does it matter now?'

'I've explained why. I don't like remembering the bad times when he's dead and she's all shocked.'

'I don't like asking, but someone may have murdered him and I have to find out the truth.'

She fiddled with the edge of the apron she was wearing. 'I was staying late because of something I had to finish and perhaps they cannot have known I was still there. I was upstairs and I could hear them because the door of the sitting room was open. Their voices got louder, then the señora came out into the hall, the señor followed her and they shouted.'

'What was their problem?'

'How could I know when I understand only a little English and they were speaking as quickly as a Madrileño after three glasses of wine?'

'So you've no idea what the row was about?'

'I've said. But most likely she'd at last found out about the women he had along when she wasn't at home.'

'Did the row reach the point where he hit her?'

'If so, it was not hard. She didn't scream.'

'Did you see her later that day?'

'Must have done.'

'Did she show any signs of injury?'

'No.'

He offered her a cigarette, she refused; he lit one. 'You've seen the women who came here when the señora was away?'

'Some.'

'Can you name any of them?'

'No. But . . . Maybe the one with the dog lives near where I do.'

'Where's that?'

'Carrer Sant Pio.'

'Tell me about her.'

'Just see her most mornings when I start off to come here.'

'Which is when?'

'Before half past seven so as I get here to work by eight.'

'And you've no idea who she is?'

'Only that she walks a black ratter.'

A dog, the size of a miniature pinscher, unrecognized by the international dog world, lively, impudent; he would have had one were Dolores not so house-proud.

He thanked Carolina for her help, returned to the station. He sat at his desk, lit a cigarette. Had he, or hadn't he, been given a lead to the identity of one of Picare's women? Were she married, had her husband suspected her adultery with Picare?

He stubbed out the cigarette. If the dog was walked every day, as was likely, the owner surely might be identified. But that would require him to be in Carrer Sant Pio early in the morning.

He dialled Llueso policia. 'Inspector Alvarez . . .' he began.

'The pearl of Spanish justice, the scourge of villains, the epitome of success.'

'Haven't you been sacked yet? How are things going for you, Emilio?'

'Well before you rang.'

'I need your help.'

'Why else would you be bothered to talk to a mere policia?'

'The problem needs a bit of explaining and that's best done over a glass.'

'Who'll be paying?'

'Me.'

'Then you're in trouble.'

'How about Club Llueso in fifteen minutes?'

Twenty minutes later, they were seated at one of the window tables in the bar. Alvarez drank, put his glass down on the table. 'It's the Picare case.'

'Drowned in his Olympic-sized swimming pool. But with you calling for help, he didn't drown accidentally and you need someone to do your job for you.'

'He'd been entertaining other men's wives.'

'In the pool? Gives a new twist to "Would you like to join me for a swim?".'

'I need to identify as many of his women as possible.'

'To console them?'

'And there's a chance of naming one by keeping watch. At the worst, it won't need more than a couple of mornings.'

'And you'd keep watch but it would be bad for your health? My lads are working too long already to be of any use to you.'

'This may be a murder case.'

'Tell me when you're certain and I'll see if I can do anything for you.' Emilio Grimalt turned his glass upside down.

Alvarez signalled to Roca for fresh drinks. He quickly explained what he wanted, drank quickly to avoid the necessity of a third round.

FIVE

After phoning eight *abogados* without any luck, Alvarez spoke to Pereyra who, in typical lawyer stalling-mode eventually admitted he might have prepared Neil Picare's Spanish will.

'Will you give me the relevant details, please.'

'Over the phone?'

'Why not?'

'I begin to wonder if you are a member of the cuerpo.'

'You want my ID number?'

'Not over the phone.'

'As you must be aware, this is a very important and urgent matter.'

'It may possibly affect the highest on the island, but that can't alter the necessity of your coming here to prove yourself before I can give you the information you seek.' The line went dead.

He replaced the receiver. Some people took their jobs far too seriously. He stared through the window at the buildings on the other side of the road. Any drive in a car in summer without air-conditioning was unwelcome, yet still preferable to working in an office. Yet it was nearing five o'clock so better to leave the visit until the next day. But like all lawyers, *abogados* made far too much money so it was reasonable to assume Pereyra would not be in his office tomorrow. He would wait until Monday.

Pereyra looked like a lawyer who would question a question. He had a balding head, beady eyes, a straight mouth, a pointed chin; he wore a suit and his tie was perfectly knotted. 'I should like to see your papers.'

Alvarez showed him the necessary identification.

'Very well.' He handed the ID card back and in order to do so, his stomach came up against the edge of the desk.

No *abogado* had ever died from starvation, Alvarez thought.

'It would have saved trouble had you come straight here rather than first phoning.'

'You meet many who falsely claim to be with the cuerpo?'

'Protection of a client and his interests are paramount.'

'Since he is dead, what would one be protecting him from?'

'Do I understand correctly that your being here means my client did not die accidentally?'

'That is what we are trying to determine.'

'You believe the contents of his will may assist you in reaching a conclusion?'

'My superior is of that impression.'

'Then he should have been in touch with me. There is a form of procedure which should always be observed. Perhaps you will inform your superior of that.'

'Perhaps' was the correct word. 'I will not forget, señor. If I may see the will?'

Pereyra picked up one of three folders on his desk, opened it and carefully checked the contents, passed across six pages bound together, the initial one being stamped with the *abogado*'s warrant. 'The will was originally drawn up in English, then the certified copy in Spanish.'

The will had been drawn up and registered three years before. The property Vista Bonita, its contents and his capital were left to his wife, Cecily Mary, with the excpetion of legacies – relatively small – to the staff in his employment at the time of his death; and a gift of ten thousand pounds to James Russell.

Attached to the will was a record of the latest value of his portfolio – large enough to allow a man to divert all the darts of fate except that of death. 'Quite an estate!'

'By some standards.'

'You handle many greater ones?'

'You would not expect me to answer that.'

A second's thought would have told him he shouldn't.

'Yes?' Ángela Torres asked, staccato style.

'Inspector Alvarez.'

'The superior chief is not in his office at present.'

'Still not back from his meal?'

'You will not appreciate that for some, work is more important than self-gratification.'

'I'll ring again later.'

'Six o'clock.'

'I may not be able to phone that late since I am meeting a man who, hopefully, will be able to identify whoever is now smuggling two brands of whisky and one of gin.'

'It is possible the superior chief will comment on the frequency with which you need to be away from the office very early in the evening in order to speak to a potential smuggler.'

'If that has happened more than once before, it's pure coincidence.'

'Might not unlikely repetition be more accurate?'

He leaned back into his chair. Women should never have been admitted to work for the cuerpo or any other police force since their minds were limited and twisted everything.

He rang Palma.

'Yes?' Salas demanded.

He identified himself.

'Your reason for calling now?'

'Because you weren't there, señor.'

'Where?'

'Where you are.'

'Are you drunk?'

'I would never consider touching liquor when on duty, señor.'

'Then you are unaware that the purpose of speech is to communicate.'

'I thought you would understand that when I said where you are, that meant where you would have been, had you been there.'

'You will not pursue the matter into total chaos. You will explain in the simplest possible manner why you are phoning me now.'

'To report what I have learned so far.'

'I will assume you are referring to the Picare case in order to prevent having to spend half an hour deciphering what you have said. Make your report.'

Alvarez repeated what Rosalía had told him and what he had learned from the *abogado*.

'A man of such unsavoury character as Picare should never have been allowed into Spain.'

'I agree, señor.'

'When I require your opinion, I will ask for it. What are the terms of the will?'

'His property and capital, with the exception of bequests, go to his wife. The largest bequest is ten thousand pounds to a friend; the remainder are relatively small.'

'His total assets?'

'His investments were recently valued at two million five hundred thousand pounds.'

'Which is how much in euros?'

He should have expected to be asked that question. 'I haven't yet received an official conversion figure.' The truth could sometimes be a good defence. 'Perhaps the exchange rate is in doubt.'

'The value of the property?'

'Three hundred and fifty thousand euros. Values have dropped, but I would still have expected it to be worth considerably more since it has a position and views to die for.'

'You can explain how one dies for a view?'

'I suppose if one walks across the lawn to get as near the view as possible, one could fall over what is virtually a cliff . . .'

'It amuses you to speak absurdly, but it suggests to me that you should be examined by a specialist. I have to wonder if you have appreciated that now there is a known motive for Picare's death?'

'I could not miss that fact, señor.'

'You tend to overrate your abilities. Can you name others with motives?'

'A cuckolded husband of which there are many.'

'Their names?'

'I cannot yet say.'

'It has not occurred to you, it is necessary to identify them even, as to be expected, you perceive sex as providing a major motive?'

'In many cases, that is the initial and primary cause.'

'Unfortunately, sex does play a mistaken part in those who live ill-adjusted lives. Money, because it is important to everyone, therefore provides a far stronger motive. At present, you will consider Señora Picare to be the main suspect for the murder of her husband if he was murdered.'

'Can one have a main suspect until one is certain a crime has been suspected, señor?'

'You will find your life far less confusing if you refrain from considering matters beyond your understanding.'

'There seems to be no reason for the señora to have wished to kill her husband. Their marriage was not blissfully happy, but after a few months, is any? There is no suspicion, no suggestion, of another man.'

'She may have been in trouble, the nature of which has not yet surfaced.'

'Such as what?'

'Addiction to a narcotic.'

'Very unlikely.'

'What is doubtful to a closed mind will be accepted as very possible to an open mind. Further, when there is a motive for killing someone, the nature of whose death cannot be immediately determined, it is reasonable to consider murder. The person most likely to benefit financially from Picare's death, in the absence of contrary evidence, must be deemed a possible murderer. You will question the señora despite any attempt by her to avoid this on the plea of shock and grief.'

'Is the señora fully conscious?' Alvarez asked Rosalía as he stood in the hall of Vista Bonita which was brilliantly lit by the sunlight coming through the rondel.

'Why do you want to know?'

'I must ask her a few questions.'

'With her husband not yet buried? Don't be absurd.'

'I'm afraid it's necessary.'

'Because you say so?'

'Those are my orders.'

'You lot don't know the word "sympathy".'

Authority was a lot less respected than it had been, as he often had cause to regret, but he admired her for challenging him even if, being a woman, she should have done so less forcefully. 'Will you find out if she can speak to me?'

'And if she says she can't, you'll drag her off to jail?'

'You seem to think we lack all sympathy.'

'You finally understand that?' She turned and crossed the hall.

He watched her climb the stairs, turn to the right and go out of sight.

She returned. 'She's said she'll try to speak to you, but only for a minute or two. She's in bed, so I've made certain she's decently covered.'

'You think—'

She interrupted him. 'Up the stairs, second door on your right. I've told her to press the bell the moment you begin to worry her.'

'I'm surprised you don't want to be in the bedroom to see I don't molest her in any way.'

He climbed the stairs, entered the very large bedroom which faced the bay; elaborately over-furnished and without taste, was his verdict. Cecily Picare, a shawl over her shoulders, lay in a king-size bed; a single sheet was pulled up to the base of her neck. A chair had been placed well away from the bed. He introduced himself, apologised for the intrusion, sat.

Her face was blowsy; whatever attraction it had once possessed was lost in the excess flesh that was veined and rough. The sheet outlined a body which possessed shape, but not one that a woman would welcome.

He remembered her husband's absurd claim to gentility. 'I apologise deeply for disturbing you, Doña. I will be as brief as possible.'

She looked past him.

'I have to ask if you can help me understand why Don Picare so sadly and tragically drowned in the swimming pool.'

'How can I?' Her voice was shaky. She had closed her eyes.

'Was he suffering from any complaint which might have caused him suddenly to be unable to swim?'

'He must have had a heart attack.'

'The medical evidence is against that possibility. Was he a strong swimmer?'

'He . . . he'd never swum before we came here . . . So busy.'

There was a pause before she continued and when she did, she seemed to have gained strength. 'He wouldn't have had a pool except it was here when we bought. I said he should learn to swim and have someone along to teach him, but he wouldn't. He liked to get in when it was so hot, but always kept the water low so he was never out of his depth.'

'Are the tiles on the bottom of the pool slippery?'

'No.'

'Have you ever slipped when in the pool?'

'I suppose I may have. If one is having fun, splashing around, one forgets to be careful.'

'Did he ever say he was worried about something; did he ever have a bitter row with someone?'

She shook her head, reached under the bottom pillow and brought out a handkerchief, wiped her eyes.

He was stamping on a grave. He apologised again, thanked her, left.

SIX

Dolores was in the kitchen, washing up the supper plates, knives and forks. In the dining room, Jaime drained his glass, refilled it, passed the bottle across to Alvarez before he noticed the other's glass was still nearly full. 'Are you all right?'

Alvarez did not answer.

Dolores looked through the bead curtain, concerned, as always, if it seemed a member of the family was not well or in trouble. 'What's wrong?' she asked.

'Enrique's not normal,' Jaime answered.

'What do you mean?'

'He's hardly said a word, stares at nothing, hasn't smoked and hardly drunk anything.'

'For you, normality is measured by the quantity of one's eating, drinking and smoking?' She stared at Alvarez. 'But it is true he did not eat as much as I had expected, even though the *alberginies farcides* were delicious. Enrique, are you not well?'

He looked up. 'I'm fine. And the stuffed aubergines were a revelation straight from heaven.'

'The why did you not eat more?'

'The children were first to what was left.'

'Did I not ask if you or Jaime wanted more before I allowed them to help themselves? And why are you not drinking?'

'I've been trying to work something out.' He picked up his glass, drained and refilled it. Jaime reached across the table for the bottle.

'There is no need for you to have any more,' she said sharply. 'There is nothing wrong with you.'

'Enrique told you he was all right, but you encouraged him to have another coñac.'

'He needs cheering up.'

'So do I.'

'Then you can come and talk as you help me with the rest of the washing-up.' She withdrew.

'Alberto was right,' Jaime muttered. 'Drink your fill before you marry because afterwards you'll always be thirsty . . . Exchange glasses. Then if she hears you filling yours again, she won't object.'

Alvarez did not move.

'You'd stand and watch a blind man walk across the auto route. I suppose you're thinking of women again?'

'Only one.'

'Can't get her out of your head?'

'It's strange. At first meeting, she's ordinary. At the second one, you begin to think there's a fire underneath. The third time, you're sure there is. It's not the wrapping that matters, but what's below.'

'If things are so desperate, go along to the house with green shutters and gain some peace or you'll have Dolores wondering and worrying.'

'She's a sleeping volcano.'

'And you need dousing. Take things more calmly or it'll all end in disaster. They always like to start off by being intriguing and making you think you've been optimistic. And are you sure you're not asking for trouble, her being so young?'

'She's not young.'

'But . . . who are you talking about?'

'The cook.'

'You could stop confusion if you would speak sensibly.'

'You sound like the superior chief.'

'And you sound like a seventy-year-old remembering his youth. Where is she?'

'Probably at home.'

'Not her, Dolores.'

'Judging by the sounds, in the kitchen.'

'Then pass the bottle over.'

Jaime poured cautiously, returned the bottle to Alvarez's side of the table. 'You have the devil's own luck. I meet someone and she's yesterday's leftover, you meet a woman and she's the dish of the day.'

'And what is the dish of the day?' Dolores asked as she came through from the kitchen with a vase in which she had arranged some flowers.

Alvarez answered before Jaime could unintentionally annoy her with an unlikely answer. 'Your *Verats fregits amb esclata-sangs, ram i magranes.*'

'Your choice is a good one. As soon as I can, I will buy some fresh mackerel.'

'You cheer me up even more than would another coñac.'

'Then there is no need for you to have another.'

Jaime sniggered.

'Yes?' Salas said.

'I have spoken to Señora Picare,' Alvarez answered.

'Well?'

'She is in a state of shock.'

'As she would expect you to expect.'

'I judged her emotion to be genuine.'

'As she hoped you would.'

'I asked her about the state of health of her late husband.'

'Her reply?'

'He was not a strong swimmer and the pool was kept shallow so that he would never be out of his depth. He suffered from no complaint, of which she was aware, that might suddenly have caused him to lose consciousness or the ability to save himself.'

'Is that all?'

'Yes, señor.'

'The range of your questioning could well have been wider.'

'She was under considerable stress and every question which I asked and she answered increased that.'

'In such circumstances, a witness is more likely to speak the truth, forgetting her intended lies.'

'If Señor Picare was deliberately drowned by someone, his wife could have had no part in the murder.'

'Do you have an acceptable reason for so firm a declaration of her innocence?'

'While questioning her, she said that because he did not swim, she thought of having the pool filled in. Had she done so, he could not have drowned. That thought made her weep as if heaven had closed its gates.'

'Someone of such limited literary ability as you should forgo fanciful similes for fear, as in this case, of saying the opposite of what was intended. Had heaven closed its gates, it would be because she was a murderess.'

'Her tears were genuine.'

'A woman uses tears as a camouflage. You will question her again, far more thoroughly; you will disregard a cataract of tears; you will abstain from introducing heaven into your report.'

'Wouldn't it be better, señor, considering all that has happened, if I wait a little . . .'

'You will determine as quickly as possible if she was in great need of more money than her husband was likely to give her, if she was having an affair and her husband had discovered this and had promised to throw her out of home and disinherit her.'

'Would he have done so when his own affairs were legion? The doctrine of equality of the sexes has thankfully not yet reached the stage where a woman has the right to claim a man's infidelities automatically negate hers. I should make the point that there has not been a single suggestion she has committed adultery.'

'You have questioned the staff as to that?'

'Not directly, but they would inevitably have remarked about the possibility had there been any such suggestion.'

'Your trust in the loyalty of an employee is today, sadly, unfounded. Have you spoken to friends and acquaintances, in particular female ones, who may have suspected such a relationship?'

'There's not been the time—'

'The Englishman, Russell, might have used his past friend-ship with Picare to explain his frequent visits which were, perhaps, made in the hope of finding Picare absent.'

'I don't think—'

'Were you to think, you would remember Russell had lunch at Vista Bonita on the day Picare died. You will question him at the first opportunity.'

'Before the post mortem? The results of that may make it

unnecessary to question him and others you have named. If I do as you suggest—'

'As I command.'

'Since it must by now be generally known we are treating the case as one of murder, rumours will be rife and innocent persons to whom we speak may have their reputations wrongly damaged.'

'Conduct a quick and efficient investigation and there will be no such risk.'

'But if it turns out that the drowning was accidental, not murder, the cuerpo's reputation for efficiency will be damaged.'

'The man who argues against his orders is inefficient as well as insolent.'

'I was expressing an opinion, señor, not arguing.'

'From you, neither is welcome. Have I not told you that at the heart of every crime is a motive and money is the most likely motive?'

'Frequently.'

'But repetition for you does not precede comprehension. If there is someone with a strong motive for murdering Picare, is touched by the evidence, however lightly, then, lacking evidence to the contrary, it is reasonable to consider him a suspect.'

'Is that not assuming a murder because there is someone who might have a motive for committing it, then naming that person with a motive to be the murderer?'

Salas brought the conversation to an end by replacing his receiver.

Alvarez picked up a pencil and a sheet of paper, wrote down the names of people he was ordered to question; added XX to signify friends, neighbours, odds and sods who had not yet come into the frame.

The list represented hours and hours of work and frustration. One person would be out with friends on a yacht, another shopping in Palma, a third on holiday in Timbuktu . . .

He opened the bottom drawer of his desk, brought out a bottle and glass.

SEVEN

Some said there was no such thing as an inexplicable coincidence. Alvarez had reason to refute that when, as he walked towards Dr Ferrer's consulting room in the medical centre, he was accosted by the woman who had challenged him on the previous occasion.

'We are still of no account?' she said angrily. 'We live in a democracy, but you think we are still in a dictatorship and authority has the right to push the ordinary citizen aside?' She turned to face the other seated men and women who waited to see a doctor. 'He is of the guardia. When we were young, he could order us around as if we were nobodies. He could assault us and if we complained, we were called liars; he could have us imprisoned because we had been denounced, but we could not denounce him. He believes he can still do as he wishes. I say he cannot.'

Several agreed – in lower key.

The post mortem was to be held on the next day and there was no pressing reason to consult with Dr Ferrer before then. Alvarez left.

Properties in Carer Julian Gayarre sold for less than might normally be expected because halfway along the narrow road, behind what had been a typical village house, was an extension in which was the area mortuary. It's identity dated to before the Civil War and as soon as that had concluded, there had been a public demand to have it removed from within the town. There had been plans to do so, but endless bureaucratic delays ensured that nothing had been done until the financial situation ensured further, indefinite delay.

In the large air-conditioned room, Alvarez stood by the tiled wall as far away as possible from the tilting table, underneath a pod of lights, on which lay the naked body of Neil Picare. Others might have learned to regard the evidence of death

unemotionally, he could not. A noted Spanish poet had written
that no man stood alone because he was diminished by another's death. Alvarez was not only diminished, he was also scared
because he was forced to accept he was mortal and a pain in
the stomach might not be due to a rich diet, but was the
sighting shot of death.

Degner Picó was cheerful despite his profession. He removed
hair cover, mouth mask, paper gown, surgical gloves and
dropped them into a disposal bin. Alvarez walked across the
room to join him.

'Dr Ferrer was correct. He did not die from drowning,' Picó
said. 'The signs of bruising on the right ankle are no longer
apparent and beneath the skin, tissues were not crushed with
sufficient force to tear capillaries or small veins.'

'Does that mean his ankle was not gripped tightly?'

'That there is not the proof it was. The cut on the right leg
was too minor to suggest with any certainty what might have
caused it.'

'It wasn't a torn fingernail?'

'The dead man's nails were well trimmed and there was no
foreign substance under them as possibly there would be had
he struggled. For a man of his age, he was in good physical
condition and not suffering from a complaint which might
have caused a sudden loss of consciousness.'

'Then if he didn't drown, why did he die?'

'Do you smoke?'

Alvarez feared he was in for another lecture. 'Only very
occasionally.'

'This seems a good occasion. We'll go outside.'

They went out to the small area beyond the extension
which was all that remained of a garden. A solitary tree
grew in a circle of earth and five oranges, still green, grew
on it. Since Alvarez had Ducados cigarettes, he hesitated to
offer them; was gratified when Picó produced a pack of Pall
Mall.

The hint of a breeze took time to disperse the smoke; from
nearby came the sounds of two children arguing.

'There are times,' Picó said, as he held his cigarette
between fingers, 'one has to admit one cannot give an

uncontroversial answer to a question. Facts can define the
course of the path from effect back to cause, but not the
reverse.' He raised the cigarette, drew on it, exhaled.
'However, circumstances, even negative ones, can enable one
to surmise that path. A healthy man is in a swimming pool
and dies, but not from drowning. Dr Ferrer examined him
and noted minor bruising and a small cut, too insignificant
to have been deliberately caused. The victim may not have
drowned, but struggled wildly to avoid drowning; a torn nail
on another's hand – the victim's were very well trimmed –
could cause such a cut.'

'Can you surmise the path? Could a struggle have resulted
in some form of vagal inhibition?'

'Vagal inhibition. What makes you suggest that?'

'There was a case in England very many years ago when
more than one woman was murdered in a bath tub by very
sharply pulling her head under the water.'

Degner dropped the butt of his cigarette on to the ground,
dug it into the earth with the heel of a shoe. 'I suspect there
are few members of the cuerpo who can refer to that case.
You must study the course of crime in other countries?'

'When I have the time, señor.'

'Death by drowning – I now use the word in its everyday
sense – can be precipitated by the sudden and unexpected
invasion of water on the naso-pharynx or glottis. Death is
immediate. A person jumping into water will close his nostrils,
usually by will, sometimes with fingers, which is why he
survives to swim again.'

'There was a second person in the pool who grabbed Señor
Picare's ankle and dragged him down, bringing his head
underwater?'

'That is possible.'

'You're not saying that's what did happen?'

'Lacking evidence of a second person in the pool at the
time of Señor Picare's death and, as you will know, of that
second person's intention to murder, it must remain no more
than a possibility.'

That bloody motive, Alvarez thought.

* * *

He sat in his office, receiver against his ear, wondering if Salas had ever considered he might not be quite so smart and clever as he believed.

'As I remarked at the beginning of this case, it becomes a question of motive. As the pathologist could unfortunately, perhaps from lack of sufficient experience, do no more than offer possibility, motive will provide probability.'

'But not prove murder.'

'As I was about to comment. When a man or woman is shown to possess motive, he or she becomes a suspect and must be closely questioned.'

'Señor, are we not putting the cart before the horse? We cannot be certain that Señor Picare was murderously dragged under the water by a second party. Yet now to investigate everyone who may in any way benefit from his death surely assumes he was murdered.'

'I remember that, also in a confused manner, you have previously said something similar. Perhaps you wish to decide death was accidental and so avoid considerable work?'

'Señor, that is an unfair suggestion. Such a thought would never occur to me.'

'Except on the subject of work, your thoughts are unfathomable. You will question the señora again.'

'I'm sure she won't be able to tell me any more than she has.'

'You will discover whether or not you are correct. You will question the staff again and I'd be grateful if you did not now assure me that you can learn nothing from them.'

Alvarez switched off the engine, undid the seat belt, stepped out of the car. After prolonged visual enjoyment of the bay, mountains, land, he crossed to the front door of Vista Bonita, rang the bell.

Carolina opened the door. 'Back again?'

'Both by necessity and with you here, pleasure. How is the señora?'

'You have come to ask to speak to her again?'

'To speak to her.'

'Your previous visit upset her and the doctor was called. He says she is not to be troubled by anyone.'

'All I want is just—'

'You will not see her.'

That was, he decided, sufficient authority to explain to Salas why he had not spoken to the señora. He stepped into the hall. 'I'd like another word with you and Rosalía.'

'Why?'

'To find out if you can remember anything you have not previously mentioned or would like to change anything you have told me.'

'I can tell you nothing more and have no need to change anything I have said.'

'I'm sorry, but I have to carry out my orders so I have to question you again.'

They went into the staff sitting room.

'Last time, you gave me the impression that the marriage was not all that happy,' Alvarez said.

'You imagine any woman could be happy if her husband dishonours their marriage time after time?'

'She wasn't willing to put up with that?'

'Only a man such as you could ask.'

'Tell me about their most serious row.'

'I have.'

'You think he did not strike her?'

'Is that what I said?'

'Yes.'

'Then why ask again?'

The questioning was proceeding as he had expected; were he in her position, understanding she might be under suspicion, he would be as un-cooperative as she was. Give it a couple more minutes, he decided, and he'd bring things to an end and speak to Rosalía.

Rosalía sat. 'I can't spend any time here.'

'I want—' Alvarez began.

'And needn't expect to get.'

'Tell me about the marriage.'

'Whose?'

'If you're determined to be un-cooperative, we'll have to go down to the station.'

'I'll be so frightened, I'll do whatever you ask?'

'How frequent were the rows between the señor and señora?'

'How long is a piece of string?'

'Carry on like this and I'll have to arrest you for trying to pervert the course of justice.'

'Perversion attracts you?'

'How long had they slept in different beds?'

'You're fascinated by other people's sex lives?'

'It's a simple question.'

'Not made for a simple reason.'

'Have you remembered the names of some of the women he entertained?'

'Not having heard names, I can't remember them.'

'Some were married?'

'As I've said previously.'

'You can remember that much? How can you be certain they were?'

'They didn't take off their rings or had a circle of white around the third finger.'

'And some of them were English?'

'You can believe a married Spanish woman would behave so openly?'

'Why do you think so many women came here?'

'You need it explained?'

'He doesn't seem to have had a charming manner.'

'He had the charm of wealth. He could have been ninety and the women would still have been along. I've a niece who works in a jeweller in Inca. She mentioned an Englishman who frequently came into the shop and chose a necklace, ring, or bracelet which looked more expensive than it was. It turned out he was Señor Picare.'

'If they received jewellery, they were little more than putas.'

'Are you trying to sound shocked? He wasn't paying them, he was giving them gifts for the pleasure they had given him.'

'You mentioned the señor was friendly to you.'

'Did I?'

'How friendly?'

'He'd have a chat in his impossible Castilliano.'

'You've said he often nipped your bum in the morning. Was that friendliness?'

'What else?'

'Depends where else he nipped.'

'You can't lift your mind off the subject.'

'He tried to get too friendly with Marta.'

'You're quite old so will know youth can become irresistible to you.'

'I'm not old.'

'It's your looks and manner which makes you seem so? But perhaps that does not need to trouble you too much. The word "inspector" makes women uneasy, yet willing because they like to be slightly in awe of a man.'

'I doubt you've ever been in awe of any man. How angry would the señora have been when she learned about the señor's entertaining habits when she wasn't at home?'

'How often are you going to ask the same question?'

'Until I get a straight answer.'

'She's not someone who'd make a spectacle of herself by anger.'

'Carolina would disagree. Did he ever try to become too friendly with you?'

'I haven't made you understand that if he'd tried anything, I'd have told him what I thought and then quit the job. Why d'you go on and on asking?'

'Because of the possibility his drowning wasn't accidental.'

'I still don't believe that.'

'Someone may have pulled him under the water.'

'When the water wasn't a metre sixty even at the deep end?'

'Done suddenly and unexpectedly, he'd have lost his balance.'

'He would have kicked himself free and stood up.'

'He could have been dead within seconds of his head being dragged under the water because of an automatic bodily response.'

'You believe he was murdered?'

'Trying to find out if he was.'

'The thought makes me . . . I need a drink.'

'To prevent you drinking on your own, I'd welcome a coñac with ice.'

She left the room, soon returned with two glasses, one of which she handed to him before she sat.

'You've said the señor entertained widely.'

'He was the last man to behave like a monk.'

'You've told me you don't know any of their names. By now, perhaps you have been able to recollect one or two?'

'If I could, I wouldn't tell you what those names are.'

'Why not?'

'Let the husbands keep their self-respect.'

'He'll know nothing unless she admits the affair to him.'

'And after you turn up and question her about the señor, he won't be suspicious?'

'I'll make him understand the reason is a totally different matter and then insist on speaking to her on our own.'

'Your lips may lie, but your eyes don't.'

'Eyes can't speak.'

'When you look at me, what they say makes me blush.'

'Very unlikely.'

'Names?'

'And if I refuse to answer, will you seize me and threaten me with dishonour if I remain dumb?'

'I would never consider such a thing,'

'It might be exciting for both of us.'

'You can find your excitement some other way.'

'Suggest one.'

'The names?'

'I'll have to whisper them.'

'Why? Who else is here but Marta?'

'She's at home.'

'Then you can shout, not whisper.'

'Despite that look in your eyes, I've been mistaken?'

He said nothing.

'Deborah Crane; Giselle Dunkling.'

'Carry on.'

'That's all.'

'I don't believe that.'

'You're being cruel. I can't think of any other names now, but I'll try and try and the next time you come here, perhaps I'll be able to tell you more.'

'Where do those two live?'

'I don't know, but Giselle probably locally. The señor collected her and drove her back and was never away for long.'

'And Deborah?'

'He was away much longer.'

'The señor wasn't worried about your seeing them?'

'He used to say the woman was a cousin, here on holiday. It seems the English would rather be thought fools than immoral.'

'Over-developed consciences.'

'You've heard there are such things?'

'What's that supposed to mean?'

'I'd whisper the answer, but you're so determined to keep away from me.' She stood. 'I want another drink. Would you like another coñac or is there something else you'd prefer? Your eyes tell me there is, but I'm a good girl.'

There was a knock on the door. 'Yes?' she said.

Marta entered, spoke nervously. 'I think I heard the señora call out.'

'I'll go and find out if she needs something. The inspector is thirsty, so show him where the drinks are.' She left.

'How are you now?' he asked Marta.

'All right,' she listlessly answered. Then said shrilly, 'He died because of me!'

'You weren't in any way responsible for what happened.'

'If I'd . . . but I . . . couldn't.'

'You must understand that what happened was no fault of yours, that you had no responsibility whatsoever. You should be proud, not troubled, that you had the good sense, the character, not to give in to his ugly suggestions.'

She briefly looked at him, then back down at the floor. 'Do . . . do you mean that?'

'I have never spoken more truly.'

She turned suddenly and hurried out. He hoped he had managed to afford her some emotional relief.

Rosalía returned. 'The señora must have cried out in her sleep. Your glass is empty again. You are very thirsty?'

'I didn't refill it.'

'Marta didn't show you where to go?'

'I didn't ask her to. I've been trying to convince her she

was in no way responsible for the señor's death by refusing his advances.'

'She's so very naive. I'll get the drinks and whilst I'm up, is there anything else you'd like?'

'What are the options?'

'Vinegar and salt crisps or Dutch cheese crunchies.'

EIGHT

Slightly breathless, despite having climbed the stairs slowly, Alvarez sat at his desk. As if by pressure contact, the phone rang.

'You have managed to reach the office this morning after being delayed by many problems?' Ángela Torres asked. 'Or perhaps you have been too busy to answer on the two previous occasions I have tried to phone you?'

'I was delayed by questioning witnesses in the Picare case, señorita.'

'The superior chief will speak to you.'

That she was not married was no cause for surprise. Only a man with masochistic tendencies would have ever considered the possibility.

'Alvarez,' Salas said sharply. 'Why have you not reported the result of your questioning of Señor Russell?'

'I haven't yet had the chance to speak to him.'

'You consider his evidence to be of no account?'

'On the contrary, señor. I decided it was best first to speak to Rosalía who is the cook at Vista Bonita.'

'You consider it necessary constantly to remind me who she is?'

'On a previous occasion, you have blamed me for not identifying the persons concerned.'

'With reason.'

'I have questioned Carolina Pellisa.'

'You have made no reference to her before. You expect me to know who she is by divination?'

'The daily who works at Vista Bonita.'

'Identify someone before you talk about him or her.'

'But you've so often . . .' He stopped. A mouse did not argue with a cat for long.

'What has she told you?'

'There are two versions regarding the state of the Picares'

marriage. Carolina's impression was that it had settled down
into the usual rut.'

'What do you mean by that?'

'A couple quieten down over the years and prefer to watch
television rather than have fun.'

'I believe you are not married.'

'No, señor.'

'Leave to others judgment on the behaviour of those who
are.'

Rumour said the Salas' marriage was far from vibrant.
'Rosalía suggests that at first the marriage was normal but
then it deteriorated and arguments were frequent and at times
so fierce that violence seemed likely.'

'How do you reconcile the two descriptions?'

'At the moment, I find that difficult.'

'You will determine which is accurate.'

'It may be rather difficult . . .'

'Were I to record the number of times you have said that,
I might well run out of numbers. You will also question, as
you should have done at the beginning, Señor Russell.'

Hotel Tamit had no claim to stars. It was two roads back from
the sea front and would not please those who sought luxury
in the bedroom, the public rooms, or *Pilotes amb safrà* with
a bottle of Vega Sicilia in the dining room.

Alvarez spoke to the receptionist who sat behind a semi-
circular counter desk. 'Señor Russell? I think I saw him go
out so he may be on the beach.'

'Can you suggest whereabouts he might have gone?'

'It's a long beach.'

He knew that. It could take a long time to find the man.
'When's lunch served here?'

'Half past one.'

To wait for Russell to return for a meal would avoid having
to search amongst tens of dozens of sunbathers and swimmers
and he might not return home in time for his lunch. The thought
of missing the meal was too unwelcome to consider. Dolores
might be cooking *Llengua de xot amb salsa*, not only one of
his favourites, but of Jaime's and the children's. He would be

left an inadequate portion for his return. 'I'll try to contact him another time.'

'If it helps, he often eats at Café Mar along the beach. Do you know him?'

'Not by sight.'

'Red, curly hair. You can't mistake him.'

Ignoring the prohibition of vehicles along the front road, he drove a few hundred metres along it, passing the large houses once owned by the wealthy from Palma who had spent much of the summers in them. The beach café had expanded from its makeshift beginning and now served simple meals at tables on the sand, each shaded by a sun umbrella. He heard Russell before identifying him; a booming laugh guided his gaze to a red-headed, bare-chested man, wearing multi-coloured swimming trunks, who sat opposite a blonde, younger than he, who wore a bikini which would not survive even a mild trimming.

He walked across the sand, which became caught up in his sandals, irritated his toes and him.

Russell had raised his glass when he noticed Alvarez approach. He lowered it.

'Señor Russell?'

He put the glass down. 'That's me.'

'Inspector Alvarez, Cuerpo General de Policia.'

'How's that?'

'A detective,' said his companion.

'Oh . . . Why?'

'I need to learn if you can in any way help me with regard to the unfortunate death of Señor Picare?'

'It was a hell of a shock to learn what had happened, but I—'

She interrupted him. She stood. 'I'll leave you two on your own.'

'No need to move,' Russell hastily said.

'I need to freshen up. See you at our table in the dining room.'

They watched her until she became lost amongst other people.

'You . . . you think I can help?' Russell asked uneasily.

'You may enable me to understand better the circumstances of what happened. Had you known Señor Picare for long?'

'Several years ago; from time back in England. I went into the local pub and he was sitting at the bar and talking to Cecily inbetween her serving drinks.'

'You became friendly with them?'

'Not right away, of course, but after a while. Frankly, I found her . . . I probably sound precious, but I don't like to hear a woman making crude innuendoes and jokes even if it's to encourage the customers to buy another drink.'

'Why d'you think they came here to live?'

'At a guess, she'd more than one man eager to show her his garden. But Neil sold his farm to a developer for a fortune and she gave him the thumbs up. They married. She wanted to live somewhere with better weather and eventually he agreed and they ended up here. You're interested in all that?'

'I like to learn as much as I can.'

'There's a rumour going around that he didn't just drown.'

'The water in the pool was kept low so that he could never be out of his depth. A post mortem has shown he suffered no illness which was likely to have caused a sudden unconsciousness or incapacity.'

Russell leaned back in the chair and the sunshine escaped the edge of the umbrella and covered the lower half of his face. He moved to his left. 'I sunburn easily and got caught the other day. The air is so clear, one doesn't realise the damage the sun can cause. I've been told that local doctors and chemists call it their patron saint.' He called a waiter over. 'What will you drink, inspector?'

'I should like a coñac with just ice, please.'

Russell gave the order. As the waiter walked away, he said, 'Does you being here, asking about them, saying there was nothing medically wrong with Neil, mean rumour may for once be right and the drowning was not accidental?'

'We cannot be certain so we have to consider all possibilities. That is why I have needed to question you, but you'll be glad to know I will soon stop. Did Señor Picare know you were here on holiday or did you meet by chance?'

'I'd written to say I'd be out and would like to meet up again.'

'He didn't invite you to stay at Vista Bonita?'

'Unfortunately not – it would have been a sight more comfortable than the hotel. I expect Cecily put the dampers on that possibility. Still, I was invited to supper, which she called dinner, on my first evening. Not that she wasn't a bit frosty.'

'Would you describe their marriage as happy?'

'Reasonably so. Cecily wanted to live a far more social life than he did which may have caused a few upsets, but I don't know.'

'Otherwise all was calm?'

'As far as I could tell.'

'Why do you think that dinner was not a success?'

'Neil and I talked about old times, she became bored and left, he opened another bottle. Pretty soon, he said that if he was given the option, he'd go back to farming. I laughed, made some comment about being careful or his wishes might come true and that got him talking. Despite all Cecily's ribald behaviour behind the bar back in England, she was unenthusiastic about making the bed springs squeak and demanded her own bedroom. He'd wondered if she was two-timing him and even employed a private detective to check up on her. Result was completely negative.'

'Do you know if you are named in the señor's will?'

'He did once say he'd leave me something for old time's sake.'

'You are to receive a legacy of ten thousand pounds.'

'Ten . . . ten thousand?'

'You are surprised?'

'I'm gobsmacked. I thought he was talking about a couple of hundred . . .' He stopped, stared at Alvarez. 'Are you now wondering if I'm sufficiently broke to have thought it a good idea to drown him since he had said what he'd leave me and I was desperate for the money?'

'I have not considered the question until now. Since it is you who have raised the possibility, did you kill him?'

'Christ, no! Don't you understand, we were friends?'

'If Señor Picare became convinced his wife was not having an affair, was their relationship as before?'

'No.'

'Do you understand why not?'

'I assumed he couldn't wholly believe the report the detective had given him, his suspicion had upset her too much for a full reconciliation, or, more likely, she knew full well how much he was having on the side'

'Did he ever mention divorce?'

'No. But if he had, I reckon he'd have said that it was better to try to put up with things rather than have to give her most of his money because the courts always favour the wife. He hadn't got used to big money and still thought like a small farmer. He'd suggest we went out to a café and it would be a case of his round, my round.'

As it should be now, but wouldn't, Alvarez thought. 'You were at Vista Bonita the day he died.'

'And he was alive when I left.'

'You didn't say goodbye to the señora?'

'I presumed she was still out and anyway I was too thoughtful to annoy her and find out.'

'Why would a normal courtesy do that?'

'She regards me as a baleful influence. I'm not wealthy and fail to corroborate her in public when she says his farm was over four hundred acres of prime grazing land and his home-bred cows won many awards at agricultural shows.'

'Did he have many friends here?'

'Fewer than he would have done if on his own.'

'He still seemed to enjoy himself?'

'With the women. When you talked about friends, I thought of men or couples.'

'You'll have met several of his female friends.'

'He wasn't generous.'

'You didn't meet any of them?'

'Only one.'

'Her name?'

'Can't remember.'

'Think harder.'

'At the moment, all I can tell you is that she came out to the island after her husband died. She put on a soulful face and Neil took her to a meal at the Residencia to cheer her up. That will have got her thinking of diamonds.'

'She had an affair with Señor Picare shortly after her husband died?'

'She had lived in Essex.'

'Why should that explain anything?'

'The devil once stayed there, but found conditions so extreme he hurried back to hell.'

'Is she still on the island?'

'I think she rents a flat.'

'Where?'

'I'm not certain. Incidentally, I've remembered her name. Lynette.'

'Her surname?'

'Hasn't yet returned to my memory.'

'Give me some more names.'

'She's the only one from his coven I met.'

'You never learned through her – women find it difficult to keep such information to themselves – who were his other female interests?'

'Not after I took her to a meal at a local restaurant and she mentioned to Neil what poor quality the food had been.'

'Was he annoyed to learn you'd taken her out?'

'He called it a sparrow challenging a golden eagle.'

'Rather humiliating for you?'

Russell shrugged his shoulders.

'Is there anything more you can tell me which might be of consequence?'

'Absolutely nothing.'

'Then I have no need to trouble you further. Thank you for your help.'

It was almost nineteen hundred hours when Alvarez once again parked in front of Vista Bonita. Rosalía opened the front door.

'What d'you want?' she asked.

'I'll tell you if no one else is listening.'

'You're full of hopeless optimism for a man who won't see fifty again.'

'I'm still in my early thirties.'

'And you believe in fairies.'

'I'm here to have a word with Marta.'

'You're wasting your time. She's at home.'

'Is she still depressed?'

'Naturally.'

'Is the señora here?'

'She's away.'

'Then at least she's better. So you're on your own.'

'And going to remain so.'

'What are you preparing for supper?'

'*Escaldums de vigilància.*'

Chickpeas – even Dolores has some difficulty in making them into a dish to enjoy. 'No doubt they'll be delicious.'

'You'll never know.'

'Where does Marta live?'

'With her parents.'

'And they live where?'

'You think she wants you around when she's at the bottom of everything?'

'Probably not, but I have to have a word with her.'

'Why?'

'To confirm or deny what I've been told. I'll be as brief as I possibly can.'

'I don't remember the address.'

'It'll be written down somewhere in case someone wants to get in touch with her.'

'Could be, I suppose,' she said reluctantly.

'Have a search for it.'

'Then you stay right here.'

'Why are you so suspicious?'

'Your eyes are more truthful than your tongue.'

'You must feel very flattered.'

'I was eleven when I learned a man's flattery has only one target. Do you stay where you are or do I forget where to look for the address?'

'You're a hard woman.'

'Far less trouble than a man who's hard.'

He watched her walk across the hall to a small table under which were telephone directories and a notebook of personal addresses and phone numbers.

She returned, handed him a small square of paper on which

she had written an address and number. 'That's everything, so there's no need to stay.'

He returned to his car. Women were suffering from hedonism when they thought men were always lusting after them.

Ca'n Porta was a casita which had been enlarged in weathered stone to provide the amenities of modern life as opposed to the basic necessities of the past. A number of roof tiles had not yet been degraded to a dull, blotched colour by the weather and showed that the enlargement had been fairly recent. The door was opened by Eva Amengual who epitomised the traditional older Mallorquin woman. She honoured the past, was a little overweight but not obese, her features expressed determination leavened by a touch of humour, her manner was direct, some-times overbearing. She spoke Castilian with occasional difficulty because her youth had been spent during the suppression of Mallorquin which had banished the language to the home or conversations with fellow, trusted Mallorquins.

'I should like to talk to Marta . . .' he began.

'She cannot speak to you,' she replied sharply.

'I know she's very unhappy.'

'And yet you think to disturb her further?'

'I fear I have to.'

'You consider yourself of greater authority than her mother?'

'Because, unfortunately, Señor Picare died—'

'Death was never more deserved. Marta was betrayed by the Englishman, as Spaniards always have been.'

'She is young . . .'

'I need to be told how old she is when I bore her in great pain?'

'I'm trying to say that time will slowly lessen her sorrow.'

'You speak as a man who cares nothing for the troubles of others.'

'I understand them because I have known great sorrow.'

'Yet you work for the cuerpo who provide sorrow?'

'I have suffered in the past as Marta now does, so will do everything to avoid bringing her more pain, but I have to speak to her for a few minutes . . .'

He stopped as Marta walked into the entrada. Her eyes were moist, her cheeks damp, her expression sad and bitter.

'Return to your room, love,' her mother said.

'What does he want?'

'To talk to you. I have told him, he cannot.'

'Marta,' he said, 'I'm very sorry to have to be here—'

She interrupted him. 'It was my fault.' Her voice was high.

'He did not kill himself, so it cannot have been your fault.'

'You say that to make me think . . . that . . .'

'I promise you, in the name of the saint of my birthday, that I speak the truth.' He hoped he would not be asked to name the saint. 'The señor was killed by someone.'

Tears dribbled down her cheeks as she ran out of the room.

'Her sorrow will lessen since you have told her that?' Eva asked with angry sarcasm.

'Is it not kinder to speak the truth than to let her continue to believe she was in any way responsible for his death?'

'I . . . I don't know.' She sat on the solitary chair. 'Why did she go and work there?' she wailed.

'Life can become more bitter than an unripe Seville orange. I will leave, but circumstances are beyond me and I will have to return tomorrow to speak to Marta.'

'You will not be welcome.'

Eva was much less antagonistic the following day. She offered him a glass of wine. They sat in the main room and after a while, to her mother's uneasiness, Marta joined them.

'I know it must distress you,' he said to her, 'but I must ask you to tell me what happened that day. Take as long as you like. If you find it becomes too difficult, we will have a break.'

Eva corrected him. 'I will say when to stop.'

She'd tell a bishop he was talking nonsense, he thought admiringly. 'Marta, Señor Russell was at the house, wasn't he?'

She nodded.

'Do you remember what they ate?'

She hesitated only briefly. '*Guàtleres amb pa.*'

'Did you have some later with Rosalía?'

She nodded again.

'Were they delicious?'

'She cooked them.'

A guarantee. Quail could somewhat lack in taste, but given a touch of salt and lemon juice before being browned in hot olive oil, cooked in a mélange of lemon juice, sweet paprika, marjoram, and parsley, wrapped in bacon, they became a gourmet's choice. 'When did you leave and return here?'

She brushed her eyes with a crooked forefinger. 'Like always, after me and Rosalía had cleaned up. The señora wanted everything spotless and back where it should be before we finished work.'

'Then you didn't see Señor Russell again?'

'Him and the señor came into the kitchen to say how much they'd enjoyed the meal. She can only say what's wrong.'

'Señor Russell left before you'd finished the work, so that would be the last you saw of him?'

'Just heard him driving off.'

'That's all you can ask,' Eva said sharply. 'Clear off and leave us alone.'

'I only have one more question and promise it won't upset Marta any more.'

'Your promise isn't worth a single centimo.'

'Marta, how do you know the señor said goodbye to Señor Russell before he drove away?'

'I heard him.'

He thanked her for finding the courage to talk to him, Eva for her patience, left.

NINE

'It is kind of you to take the trouble to get in touch with me,' Salas said sarcastically.

'Señor,' Alvarez began, 'I have—'

'I hope you are not about to say you have tried to phone me several times and received no answer; there was no connexion due to Telecom's incompetence; your mobile seems to have broken; you met a man who told you he had very important information, but after a long and liquid conversation you decided he was mentally deficient?'

'I have spoken to Señoritas Marta Espinar and Rosalía Mulet and their evidence is slightly at odds.'

'As you have already told me. The nature of your questioning may have made that inevitable.'

'The question is whether or not Señor Russell left Vista Bonita when Señor Picare was still alive. In effect, Marta says he did, Rosalía that he did not. Marta unfortunately believes the señor intended to divorce his wife in order to marry her and—'

'There is no need to repeat something you have already told me.'

'Minds are often clouded by emotion.'

'What are you attempting to say?'

'If Marta believed Señor Russell might be thought responsible for the señor's death, perhaps a sense of responsibility would have urged her to free him from suspicion.'

'Russell has also been troubling her?'

'There's no reason to think so.'

'Then why should she suffer any wish to make up the story?'

'I don't think she did.'

'We seem to have become disconnected even though we are still speaking.'

'I'm trying to present all sides.'

'And presenting nothing. Do you or don't you believe Marta's evidence'

'Since it was necessary to determine whether her personal distress was disturbing her memory, I asked her what she ate at lunch that day. Her answer corroborated what Rosalía had said she cooked. Quail, seasoned with—'

'I am uninterested.'

'It can be a truly delicious dish.'

'You failed to hear what I said?'

'Since Marta accurately remembered what they'd eaten, I accepted it was reasonable to accept her evidence about what happened. Russell left Vista Bonita after lunch and when the señor was still alive.'

'Russell may have been in the pool with Picare.'

'Hardly likely since she heard them saying goodbye.'

'Where was she when she heard them?'

'In the kitchen,'

'Have you checked that the sound of voices would have reached her there?'

'It is my intention to do so as soon as I have reported, señor. He drove away immediately afterwards.'

'As to be expected if he'd murdered Picare.'

'His clothes would have been sodden.'

'That would not have prevented his leaving.'

'There wasn't enough time for all that after Marta heard them say goodbye.'

'She may be misjudging the length of the interval between hearing the voices and Russell's driving off. It would be normal for a woman to misjudge time.'

'If he had been clothed in the pool, there would have been considerable noise when he got out and the water streamed off him. She would have heard that.'

'Not necessarily. As you will have reason to appreciate, a wandering mind misses much.'

'Señor, I will return to Vista Bonita and check what, when one is in the kitchen, one can hear from the pool.'

'Something which should have been done before.'

Rosalía's words were sharp. 'What brings you back yet again?'

'You,' Alvarez answered.

'Then you're a born loser.'

'I need your help.'

'To do what?'

'Talk while I'm in the kitchen and—'

'Forget it.'

'And you're out by the pool.'

'Why?'

'I want to make certain I can hear you speak.'

'Why?'

'Marta says she could hear the señor and Señor Russell say goodbye.'

'With her mind in its recent state, it's surprising she didn't think she was hearing visitors from space.'

'Would you go through to the pool and speak at three or four places around it?'

'If I must.'

'You'll have my gratitude.'

'Which heads the list of what I least desire.'

'Where is the kitchen?'

She pointed. 'First on the right. And don't touch anything on the table.'

'What are you preparing to cook?'

'Can't you think of anything but food? A stupid question. Food comes second on your list of what you most want.'

He walked down a brief passage, turned into the kitchen which seemed to possess every culinary device which had been invented. He looked at the bowls and dishes on the central table and tried to guess from their contents what could be for lunch. *Tonyina amb safrà*? Or the saffron in a very small container could suggest fish.

Rosalía returned. 'Have you lost your voice?' he asked.

'You didn't hear me?'

'No.'

'I didn't shout because I was reluctant for anyone but you to learn why I'd enjoy being with a very mature man.'

'You must go back and try again.'

'When I've too much work to waste more time. And a lady only admits to the unmentionable once.' She smiled mockingly.

* * *

Alvarez held the receiver to his ear and gloomily accepted he faced one more of life's injustices. If he left Salas waiting on the phone, he received a lecture on unnecessary delay. If he now complained about the waste of several minutes of his time . . .

'Yes?'

'I am just back from checking whether someone by the pool could be heard in the kitchen, señor.'

'Did I know what you are talking about, I might be able to appreciate the value of what you will have learned.'

'I went to Vista Bonita to learn if Marta in the kitchen would have heard Russell say goodbye to Señor Picare in the pool. I asked Rosalía to stand at various places around the pool and speak as if to someone were near her, while I remained in the kitchen. Unfortunately, I could not hear a single word.'

'Why is that unfortunate?'

'It suggests Marta's evidence has to be wrong. There is the possibility, even the probability, she is so convinced even now that she is in some way responsible for the señor's death, that her evidence cannot unequivocally be accepted.'

'It did not occur to you that were Russell and the señor by the pool, their voices would carry more firmly than a woman's? What you offer as evidence is of doubtful value.'

'On the contrary—'

'You need to learn you should never interrupt a senior officer.'

'Señor, I was trying to explain why you were wrong.'

'When you are unable to understand what I say, you will respectfully ask me to repeat my words in simpler form.'

'I did understand, but I didn't think you did.'

'Your inability to take advantage of advice is remarkable.'

'I understood the problem you have just mentioned and had dealt with it. After I failed to hear Rosalía, I went out to the pool and she stayed in the kitchen. She could not hear me.'

'Had you mentioned this, you would have avoided an unnecessary misunderstanding. Have you questioned Deborah Crowe and Giselle Dunkling?'

'Not yet, because of—'

'Which of your favourite excuses?'

'The truth, señor.'

Alvarez refilled his glass with brandy and ice. He drank, put down the glass on the dining-room table. 'I reckon I got the better of the superior chief earlier on.'

Jaime was watching the television. 'She won't have to spend much time on her own!'

'Who won't?'

'Stop talking and look.'

A young, sensuously beautiful woman was dancing; she wore a floral skirt which flared up each time she and her partner turned.

Not for him, Alvarez decided. Any woman so immediately attractive would choose wealth, whatever the difference in ages. So often, Jaime's tastes were impractical.

'She'd make me give up drinking.'

'Who is the magician?' came the call from the kitchen.

Jaime ignored the question. The dance ended and the couple left the floor. With one more weak joke, the show's host introduced the next couple.

'Why doesn't one ever meet someone like that?'

'Much better to meet someone less obvious.'

'You'd choose Lucia from the port?'

'Someone warm and friendly, who doesn't admire her refection every time she passes a mirror.'

'Are you on about youngsters again?'

'No.'

'You've had another slice of luck?' Jaime spoke with the annoyance of someone who was failing to enjoy what others did. 'Who's got you dreaming this time?'

'The cook at Vista Bonita.'

Jaime pointed at the bead curtain. 'She's always said you live for your stomach.'

'I wouldn't live without it. And what better way?'

'You need to be told?'

Dolores' head appeared between two strings of the bead curtain. She spoke to Jaime. 'My cooking gives you no pleasure?'

'How can you think that?'

'What do you think Enrique needs to be told?'

'I . . . I've forgotten.'

'Your memory would improve if you did not refill your glass the moment it is empty.' She withdrew.

Jaime muttered. 'She'd deny a drink to a man dying of thirst.'

'Not a drink of water.'

'She won't understand that water kills more people in the world every year than alcohol. Have you ever met a woman who can think reasonably? I suppose you'll say yes because of the new one. She can cook an old pigeon and make it taste like a capon. How many special meals have you had with her so far?'

'None.'

'Things not going as well as you'd hoped? You'd better remember the quote in *El Dia*. "Never suffer the pain of gaining what you most desire".'

'Written by someone who ended up with more than he started.'

Dolores began to sing. Jaime picked up the bottle of René Barbier and refilled his glass.

TEN

Sergeant Grimalt, policia local, phoned just after nine o'clock. Alvarez, newly arrived, used a handkerchief to clear the sweat from his face before he lifted the receiver. 'Inspector Alvarez, Cuerpo General.'

'Late to work as usual.'

'Who's that?'

'Two guesses and you're out.'

'Emilio Grimalt, since you're the only policia who has the accent of someone pretending to speak Mallorquin. Is this a social call?'

'To tell you that you've caused my lad a load of extra work.'

'Won't do him any harm,'

'It would cause you to collapse.'

'Has he been running a double marathon?'

'I wouldn't expect you to remember that you wanted to know about the woman who walked a ratter every morning at the same time. She never turned up for a couple of days, then not until nine thirty when you'd said she'd be there much earlier.'

'What's half an hour?'

'Your morning nap in the office.'

'A gross slander.'

'Truth doesn't slander. The dog-walker's name is Marie Poperen.'

'Is she French?'

'A Russian from Moscovitch.'

'You're a premature comedian.'

'The job took my lad hours and hours and you're showing as much gratitude as if it had been a five-minute doddle.'

'Where does she live?'

'A *possessió* about a kilometre and half out of Llueso on the Laraix road.'

'If that's where I think it is, the property has enough land to walk a dozen dogs, so why should she do that in the village?'

'How should I know, but women take more care over their dogs than their husbands.'

'A well-founded observation?'

'You manage to give offence even if it's not intended.'

He wrote the name, Marie Poperen, below that of Debra Crane and Giselle Dunkling. Three women who had to be interviewed to determine whether each had a husband or partner who had betrayed her and she had learned this, so providing a clear motive for the murder of Picare and the dismissal of Salas' constantly repeated opinion that money was the motive for the majority of crimes. A satisfactory conclusion to the case. But, as so often, satisfaction came at the price of work.

Sa Molet was few kilometres from Llueso, at the end of a drive which had been lined with palm trees until the destructive beetle had arrived in an imported tree; now there were young Judas trees which, even when in bloom, would fail to provide any sense of grandeur.

The house was rock built, large, and gauntly impressive. In the past, peasants had viewed it with nervous dislike – wealth meant power, power needed to impose itself on the weak in order to be powerful.

Piere Poperen was reputed to have made his fortune developing land in the south of France; his wife had been wealthy before their marriage. It should have been a recipe for happiness, but such recipes could collapse as dramatically as a soufflé.

A maid, in conventional uniform, opened one side of the massive, panelled front door.

'Is Doña Poperen here?' he asked

'You are?'

He was not being mistaken for visiting gentry. He identified himself.

'Doña Poperen is at home.'

'I should like to speak to her.'

'I will ask if she is free.'

The entrada was a high-ceilinged hall, furnished with a taste that excluded the customary aspidistras or other evergreen indoor plants.

The wait was short before he was shown into a large sitting room. Two of its bleak rock walls were softened by brightly coloured tapestries. Marie Poperen's hair was carefully styled, her make-up enhanced her features yet was all but unnoticeable; her dress, he guessed, was expensive and in the latest fashion, even if modest.

'Good morning, inspector. I understand you wish to speak to my husband. I am afraid Jacques is in Antibes.'

She spoke Spanish fluently, with only a light accent, which surprised him. The French seldom bothered with other languages, being entirely concerned with keeping their own historically, grammatically and contextually pure.

'In fact, Doña Poperen, it is you I wished to talk to.'

'Juana must have misunderstood you. There is reason to speak to me?'

The door opened and a ratter ran in, followed by Juana. The dog stopped in front of Alvarez's chair, stared at him, barked.

'Be quiet, Petite,' Juana ordered.

The dog quietened, Alvarez moved an arm, the barking recommenced. A true Mallorquin breed. No offered friendship until convinced it would be returned.

'Why is Petite in here when I have a guest?' Marie Poperen asked.

'I'm sorry, doña, but she escaped as I came to ask you if you wished for something.' Juana moved quickly, caught Petite and held her under her arm.

'You would like some coffee?' Marie asked.

'Thank you, but I think not,' Alvarez answered. Custom now dictated a drink was offered.

'Very well,' she said to Juana who left with Petite.

Alvarez started the conversation on a friendly note, despite the rejection of custom. 'A charming little dog.'

'I am very fond of her. Inspector, what brings you here?'

'As a matter of fact, to talk about Petite.'

'He has been injected against rabies.'

'I believe you regularly walk him in the village in the morning?'

'Is that forbidden?'

'I am not concerned with matters which consider dogs.'

He again tried not to sound annoyed at her muddling of importance. 'I am in the cuerpo.'

'So I was informed.'

'I need to know if you do walk him in the village?'

'Really?'

She had decided to be the grande dame. He would be direct. 'My question is this. Why should you regularly walk him in the village when there are very many hectares here in which he can run without the risk of traffic.'

'I would not expect that to concern you.'

'Is your husband often away?'

He waited, then repeated the question.

'Once again, I consider I have no need to answer.'

'You have a reason for not wishing to answer?'

'My husband travels to France several times a year for business reasons. Having answered you, please be kind enough to leave.'

'I believe you knew Señor Picare?'

'I met him.'

'Frequently?'

'What do you mean?'

'Was it once a month, once a week?'

'You expect me to remember every luncheon, every dinner to which my husband and I were invited?'

'And not to meetings when you were on your own?'

'You wish to ask something, but lack the character to do so directly? Were Neil and I lovers? Frequently, when Jacques was in France. Did he know this? Yes, as I know he returns to Antibes more often than business demands because of Denise Disault.'

'This did not concern you?'

'Why should it? Caviar is delicious, but eat it every day and one will long for a different taste.'

'Which may prove to be bitter.'

'Making the return to caviar tasty once more.'

'When will Don Poperen return?'

'When he wishes to refresh his palate.'

'You do not know?'

'Probably soon. And to celebrate our reunion, we will dine

at the new restaurant in Sineu which has a French cook . . . Have I dismayed your island morals, inspector?'

'You have explained how to lead a happy life.'

Alvarez should have known what Salas's reaction would be to his report.

'You are saying she had no hesitation in admitting both she and her husband are committing adultery and that to the knowledge of the other?'

'It seems reasonable to suppose these visits to Vista Bonita were not simply social.'

'Why?'

'A married woman on her own constantly visiting a married man whose wife is not on the island is not doing so just to be a thoughtful neighbour.'

'The conjecture of a mind which prefers guilt to innocence. What did she admit?'

'I have just explained, señor.'

'Do you believe her?'

'I see no reason not to.'

'A judgment which cannot be accepted unquestioned. She is married to her husband?'

'Would she be married to anyone else?'

'You are insolent.'

'If I had spoken as you did, señor, I am sure you would have addressed me in similar vein.'

'You will refrain from incorrectly presuming what I might say. Have you questioned her husband?'

'He is in Antibes on business and because Madame Disault lives there.'

'Who is she?'

'His little cabbage.'

'It amuses you to speak nonsense.'

'It's the French for mistress.'

'I am well aware what it means. My remark was to remind you that any attempt by you to give the impression of sophistication is unlikely to succeed. Have you requested the French police to question the husband?'

'Not yet.'

'Why not?'

'I need your authority to make the request.'

'Which would have been given had you thought to ask for it as soon as you were made aware of the regrettable circumstances.'

'Then I now have your authority, señor?'

'Yes.' Salas replaced the receiver.

Alvarez poured himself a reviver. When he saw what was left in the bottle, he made the mental note to buy more brandy at the first opportunity. He spoke on the telephone to the Interpol representative in Madrid and requested that the French police in Antibes be asked to question Poperen and learn if he was aware of his wife's adultery.

He returned home to lunch.

He awoke, levered himself upright in the chair, answered the phone call. The French police had been able to identify Mademoiselle Disault and speak to her. She had not known Monsieur Picare. Monsieur Poperen paid the rent of her flat and provided her with an allowance.

Alvarez congratulated them on the speed with which they had worked.

'We knew she lived in Antibes, so the task of identifying her was not as great as it might have been since she was the named tenant of the flat. I hope the information is of value.'

'Very much so,' he politely assured them.

'The French,' Alvarez reported to Salas, 'have identified Mademoiselle Disault and can confirm she is Poperen's mistress.'

'Would that investigations on this island were carried out as swiftly and successfully.'

'It wasn't as difficult as it might have seemed . . .'

'You would have declared the task impossible.'

'They knew she lived in Antibes; that it was likely she worked for Poperen.'

'A probability which might well have escaped you.'

'I don't think that is so, señor.'

'You discount experience?'

'She was distressed by the questioning, very likely because

she was reminded that he would no longer be financing her if Poperen had had anything to do with the death of Picare.'

'Your cynicism is unnecessary.'

'It was the person to whom I spoke who made that observation. The French are realistic in such matters. We can now dismiss the possibility that she was in any way connected with the case.'

'The reason for such conclusion?'

'Denise Disault was not married. There was no husband sufficiently outraged by her affair to murder Picare.'

'Due to the immorality which in these days has overcome morality, she may well have had another lover who discovered her illicit relationship with Picare.'

'If there were such a man, he must surely have wondered at the source of her money. With threats or observation, he would have learned about Picare. In which case, he would have accepted the situation provided he benefited.'

'The French speaker also offered that proposition?'

It seemed reasonable to agree. 'Yes, señor.'

'Their degree of mental morality is regrettable. You will ask the French authorities if she did have a lover; if so, to identify him.'

'This may well take longer than before,' he was told. 'It is unlikely she would have restricted herself to one lover, when he would frequently not be with her.'

The French, he decided, would not be bothered to pursue the investigation.

Jaime and Alvarez sat at the table after supper had finished. Dolores was washing up, the children were out, playing with friends.

'How's life?' Jaime asked, as he passed the bottle.

'Same as ever.' His glass refilled, Alvarez returned the nearly empty bottle of Valdepenas to the centre of the table. 'All work, no play and Salas shouting.'

'I wonder if he's quite the bastard you always make him out to be. What's he done this time?'

'Keeps moaning about the immorality of modern life.'

'Because he's not getting his fair share of it?'

'Probably.'

'What's so immoral?'

'A married man had a petit choux in Antibes. The wife knew about her and didn't give him hell.'

'Sounds like a marriage made in heaven.'

Dolores stepped through the bead curtain. 'Whose marriage is so fortunate?'

Alvarez hurried to answer her. 'A couple I've heard about. They live here, but he frequently goes to France on business. Some wives would be worried by the thought of what he got up to in France, but she isn't. I was telling Jaime what a remarkable woman she was.'

'Remarkable? You consider I would not trust my husband if he travelled to France without me?'

'I know your trust is complete and unshakable.'

'Would you describe my marriage as made in heaven?'

'I have always considered it to be.'

She returned into the kitchen.

Jaime spoke very quietly. 'What's she on about?'

'Seeking confirmation you've never had any regrets about marrying her.'

'Why does she get in such a state because I met Teresa by chance, suggested a drink in Bar Español and made the mistake of sitting at an outside table. Inés saw us and was on the phone to Dolores before we'd finished our drinks? You'd have thought we'd been found in bed together.'

'Many women would have considered that a future possibility.'

'That I should be so lucky!' He drank deeply.

Alvarez drove slowly along the road, three back from the sea, bordered by bungalows and houses, largely built as second homes for foreigners and now heavily taxed since the owners were not resident in Spain. Casa Mirabel was a small bungalow, similar to others, with a small front garden in which a few sad plants grew, stunted by the salty air. He rang the bell to the right of the front door. A not quite middle-aged woman opened it.

'Señora Metcalfe?' he asked

'Yes.'

That single word identified her nationality. He spoke in English, explained he wished to speak to her.

'It's about the collision we had in the car?'

'That will be dealt with by Trafico.'

'Thank God no one was hurt. The other driver kept shouting it was all my fault and he and his passenger became so excited I was grateful when a local police car came along.'

'I fear we Mallorquins can often become excited.'

'I always go around a roundabout on the outside lane. The policeman seemed to say I should have been on the inside lane and then the other car would not have hit mine. But he was overtaking so I thought he had to be at fault. Can you tell me which lane I should have been in?'

As with so many questions in Spain, they were only answered when there was need. 'You should ask a local policia.'

'I did and I don't think he knew.'

Neither did he, now that he considered the problem. 'Señora, is your husband here?'

'He's playing tennis. Doesn't matter how often I tell him that's crazy in this heat and he'll have a heart attack. He won't listen.'

He tried to lessen her fears by saying several foreigners played tennis in the summer and he knew of none who had suffered a heart attack, which was both true and an indirect lie since he would have been unlikely to hear of such an unnecessary death. 'Señora, I should like to speak to you and, later, your husband, about the tragedy concerning Señor Picare.'

'My husband must be here.'

'Why is that?'

'I need his support.'

'For a particular reason?'

'Don't you know a wife always needs her husband's support when something unexpected and unpleasant has happened? It seems with you being here, there must be some truth in the rumour that his death was not an ordinary accident.'

'We cannot be certain, but there is reason to believe it may not have been.'

'And you think we can help you? But of course we can't.'

'I have been told you were friends of his.'

'As were many other people.'

'Amongst whom there may well be someone with reason to have been unfriendly. You may be able to help me determine who such persons might be.'

'You think it may be one of us since we're foreigners? You'd believe anything of the English because of Gibraltar. But ask you where's the difference between Gibraltar and Cuela and Melila and you can't answer.'

'I assure you that I am in no way influenced by the presence of the British on Spanish land—'

'British land.'

'Let us not argue over a subject which has disturbed relations between the two great nations over so many years.'

'All right, pax. I'm afraid I became rather heated.'

'A sign of pride in one's own country, señora. I will, as you say in England, lay my cards on the table. It has become necessary to speak to ladies who knew Señor Picare.'

'Then you must be busy.'

'Did you visit him at Vista Bonita?'

'Yes.'

'When you were on your own?'

'My husband did not accompany me because he would have been bored to tears.'

Alvarez's imagination went briefly into overdrive. 'Did he know you visited Señor Picare at his home?'

'Yes. You are surprised?'

'I have to consider Señor Picare's reputation.'

'And you now think it necessary to add my name to those he "entertained"? I am dismayed and flattered. Dismayed you believe I could have been eager to betray my marriage without a second thought, flattered you consider Neil would have had the slightest lascivious interest in an aging woman.'

'Far from aging, señora.'

'Words to compensate for your over-reaching imagination? I did go to Vista Bonita quite often. And every time, I would find Neil to say hullo provided he was not entertaining in the bedroom. So now I imagine you're wondering what iniquity attracted me.'

'I would not consider such possibility.'

'A moment ago, you seemed more than ready to do so. My reason for going to Vista Bonita was far less interesting than imagination suggests. I went there for cooking lessons.'

'Cooking lessons?' he confusedly repeated.

'The cook there . . . I can never pronounce her name.'

'Rosalía Mulet.'

'I don't suppose you know she's a wonderful cook, as she's always ready to say. We have eaten there two or three times – Neil and his wife were inviting minor ex-pats to prove they were socially broad-minded. The meals could have been served in a five-star restaurant. I found out the name of the cook and went up to his place when I knew he was away. I met Rosalía, flattered her shamelessly, asked her if she would show me how to cook more interestingly than I managed. John now says I must have descended from Escoffier.'

Even when not in the cuerpo, a Mallorquin had an inbuilt tendency to look for an ulterior motive. Was he naive to accept what she said because she spoke firmly, with confidence, and must realise how easily her story could be checked? Did she present so unlikely a story in the belief that its very unlikelihood would give it credence?

'I have one last question, señora. I'm afraid it may give offence, but it has to be asked. Did Señor Picare ever attempt to seduce you?'

'When his choice was capons, not old hens?'

He stood. 'Thank you for not taking offence.'

They heard a car enter the drive. 'That will be John,' she said.

'In order not to cause any problem, señora, I will say I have been asking you about the car collision.'

'That's kind of you, but there's really no need. He's easily amused.' She called out, 'I'm in here, John, with Inspector Alvarez.'

Metcalfe entered. He was wearing a shirt with sleeves that were rolled up; he had no right arm.

ELEVEN

'I have spoken to Señora Metcalfe,' Alvarez reported over the phone.

'And?' Salas demanded.

'She is an attractive woman, rather because of her personality than her appearance. When I questioned her, she said immediately that from time to time she had visited Vista Bonita.'

'Picare was attracted by her, whatever her features, and she sold her virtue to gain the benefits of a rich man's company.'

'A very unjust judgment. She went to Vista Bonita to obtain cooking lessons.'

'That is the latest euphemism for adultery?'

'She had lessons from the cook, Rosalía.'

'She needed to be shown how to boil an egg? It is to be hoped for Señor Metcalfe's marriage that his naivety equals or surpasses yours.'

'He lost his right arm three years ago. Before then, he'd been a keen sportsman who had to restrict his eating. His wife set out to give him the most tasty cooking she could manage in an attempt, which she knew must be weak, to compensate. Her love for him was not lost along with his arm.'

'You should have presented this fact without puerile comment at the beginning.'

'I would have done so sooner had you not assumed that because Señora Metcalfe visited Vista Bonita, she must have accommodated Picare during such visits.'

'You chose to be diverted.'

'But . . .'

'You have questioned the cook to confirm Señora Metcalfe's evidence?'

'No, señor, because—'

'The need to do so has not occurred to you?'

'If Señor Metcalfe was physically incapable of dragging Picare under the water sufficiently quickly and forcefully—'

'Was he?'

'Obviously.'

'You readily and without question accept the obvious? You will get into a swimming pool and, with help, determine whether with only one arm, a man can be dragged under water with force and speed. Was Señor Metcalfe naturally right-handed? One more fact which needs to be determined.'

'Were that so, his left arm would, by now, have strengthened very considerably through constant use.'

'A supposition which must be tested. You and a second man will carry out that test in a swimming pool.'

'I'm a very poor swimmer . . .'

'Your ability does not matter since you will be the victim.'

'But to do as you suggest could be fatal.'

'You will be in a pool. The women who were deliberately drowned were in a tin bath smaller than they and their heads were pushed under the water at the same time as their legs were drawn up.'

'I hope that's a sufficient difference.'

'You will order a policia to help you.'

'He's not going to be happy if he knows he could kill me.'

'You will not mention the improbability for fear he fails to use sufficient strength.'

'If he doesn't understand what could happen, he's likely to become too enthusiastic.'

'You will not be finding out something we already know, that in certain circumstances and conditions, a sudden rush of water up the nose and mouth can prove fatal. You are merely going to find out whether a one-armed man can pull you under the water with sufficient force.'

Another difference Alvarez found difficult to accept.

Alvarez stood alongside Virgilio Veno at the edge of the council swimming pool, built five years before in an unusual decision to repay, in another form, some of the money taken in rates which would have otherwise unaccountably disappeared.

'Take it very easy,' Veno said for the fifth time to Alvarez. He had been given the role of victim despite Salas' directions.

'I'm only going to use one arm. You can't be in any danger,' Alvarez assured him.

'Ever done anything like this before?'

'No.'

'Then you can't say what could happen any more than I can. Take things really quietly or I'll make it clear what I think.'

'If something goes wrong, you won't have that chance.'

'How d'you comfort a dying man? Tell him heaven has closed its doors?'

Veno jumped into the pool, his multi-coloured trunks notice-able in the sunlight which came through the transparent roof. He was a notably good swimmer and two young women, in fairly minimal costumes by the diving boards, watched him with interest. Peacocks were useless, but they attracted attention.

Veno completed his fourth length, stood up in the shallow end. 'I'm ready, but not willing.'

Alvarez was not an enthusiastic swimmer, being well aware of the dangers water offered. He looked to check a lifeguard was on duty, found none was present.

'Come on or we'll be here until the place closes.'

He went down the steps and forward until the water was at shoulder level.

'Know what I'm going to do if you try to be too enthusi-astic?' Veno asked. 'Twist off your goulies.'

Alvarez took a deep breath, lowered himself under the water, opened his eyes. Veno's legs appeared to be more solid than he had judged them when on land. He gripped the left leg above the ankle with one hand, pulled sideways to bring the other tumbling into the water. Veno remained upright.

'Were you tickling me?' he asked as Alvarez surfaced. 'You'd better try again and put more beef into it.'

Using as much force as he could muster in the deadening effect of the water, Alvarez pulled. Veno began to lose balance and immediately kicked out with his leg to free himself.

'If you want to know if it can be made to work,' he said, when Alvarez surfaced, 'you stand and I'll pull.'

Veno had the build of a man who regularly lifted weights, ran on a moving track, used a dry-land rowing machine. 'No need to bother.'

'You've learned all you need to know?'

'Yes.'

'Then how about a couple of lengths for ten euros, you with a half-length start?'

'It's against my pocket to bet.' Alvarez climbed out of the pool and enjoyed the warm relief which came from safely completing a dangerous task.

'Señor,' he said over the phone, 'I can state that a one-armed man cannot pull another under the surface, let alone with sufficient force to drive water fiercely up the nose.'

'The basis for your statement?'

'The result of the tests you asked me to carry out.'

'Your assistant could not drag you under?'

'No, señor.'

'Very well.'

'So it's become a case of two down, three to go.'

'What is that supposed to signify?'

'I think it isn't credible to suppose Jacques Poperen would have returned from Antibes by the time of Señor Picare's death and done so unobserved.'

'Why not?'

'He was enjoying life with his mistress.'

'"Enjoy" is a word few would use, the circumstances being what they are. Have the French police reported whether or not the woman has another illicit partner who suffered what some would mistakenly term "jealousy" and came to the island?'

'I am still waiting to hear from them; I will phone them again . . . Señor, having risked my life in the swimming pool to be certain Señor Metcalfe could not have dragged Picare under the water, three suspects remain to be questioned.'

'Three?'

'Señoras Crane and Dunkling. There is also Lynette whose surname I have not yet been able to determine.'

'You choose to forget Señor Russell?'

'The legacy was to be spent on a party of remembrance. The sum was not inconsiderable, but unlikely to provide the motive for murder unless Russell was destitute. Although staying in a third-rate hotel, this was not the case. For once, it seems money is not the root of evil—'

'The love of money is the root.'

'Russell had met Lynette through Picare and decided to have a stab at her.'

'He had reason to injure her?'

'It is a Mallorquin expression and not to be taken literally.'

'Restrict yourself, if you cannot deny yourself, to local expressions which are not meaningless or misleading.'

'She rejected his advances since he could not offer her the kind of life Picare did. If money was the motive, could Russell for some reason have believed Picare had named Lynette in his will for a considerable sum which provided him with a second reason to murder Picare? A short-lived possibility as Marta's evidence made clear.'

'In what way?'

'Señor, I understand you will not wish me to repeat what I have said previously, but your question makes this inevitable. Marta heard Russell say goodbye to the señor and then the car drive away.'

'You therefore dismiss him from suspicion? Yet have you not told me that she is so naive she will believe most anything, so emotionally upset her testimony is of doubtful value? Have you questioned him as a suspect, not merely a name?'

'It seemed most unlikely he could be a suspect in view of the facts.'

'You do not understand that, as I have just pointed out, there are reasons to accept they might not be facts. Have you tried to question Debra Crane, Giselle Dunkling or Lynette . . . What is her surname?'

'Russell did not give it.'

'Because he thought that if he did, you might – how do you misphrase it – take a stab at her?'

'I would not engage in such a relationship in the normal

course of events, but as she may possibly be of assistance to us in the case, I would never begin even to consider that.'

'To deny too forcefully is to confirm.'

Alvarez arrived early, or not as late as usual, at the post. The duty cabo made a point of looking at his watch and expressing surprise.

Alvarez sat behind his desk, used a handkerchief to remove the perspiration from forehead cheeks and neck. The continuing high heat was enervating humans, harming plants and trees, threatening water supplies. A good downpour was much needed.

He stared at the sheet of paper on the desk. In his hand-writing were the names of those he had to question. Only two had been crossed off and now one of them, Russell, had to be rewritten. It was the last sack which broke the camel's back.

Debra Crane lived on the outskirts of Mestara, an ancient town on the flat plain, noted for its weekly market and skill in growing strawberries. The inhabitants' hostility to those from Llueso, for a reason that had disappeared into the past, was maintained. A Mallorquin welcomed someone or some-thing to dislike since who or which could be blamed for any present annoyance.

The stone-built, adjoined house was in appearance similar to all others in the road with the exception of the shutters which had been painted, not oiled. Alvarez rang the bell. The door was opened by a sixtyish man whose shirt was white, light-brown shorts held a crease, and sandals were newly polished. Such elegance reminded Alvarez he should have changed his shirt that morning. 'Señor Crane?' He introduced himself.

'Deuced glad you speak English or we'd have to resort to hand signals. The only Spanish I know is *vino tinto*, *rosado*, and *blanco*. Don't need any more to live well.' He laughed.

The braying of a donkey was Alvarez's judgment. An Englishman who viewed the islanders with condescension since they did so many things in a different way which marked their inferiority.

'Come on in, inspector. Rather primitive, I'm afraid, but

it's rented and only a pied-a-terre, if you know what that means.'

'There's no ground floor?'

'But you're standing . . .? Having a bit of a laugh? You've obviously a sense of humour. Must have some English blood in you, what? But you mustn't just stand there to say whatever it is you want to say, enter our humble abode.'

They went into a small sitting room, once the entrada. A middle-aged woman on the settee was knitting. She placed needles, wool, and several inches of knitting into a canvas bag.

'A visiting detective,' Señor Crane announced, 'here to find out if we robbed the local Sa Nostra bank.'

She was not the vivacious woman Alvarez had expected – before meeting her husband, that was. 'I apologise for this interruption, señora, but as I have explained to your husband, I am asking people who knew Señor Picare if they can help me.'

'He was one snooty sod!' Crane remarked. 'Didn't want to know anyone who never had a five-hundred-euro note in his pocket. They say he may have committed suicide or something. Did us all a good deed, I say.'

'Please don't talk like that, Ivor,' she said sharply.

'Because he'll think I didn't like the man and will go to hell for saying such a thing?'

'Please sit, inspector,' she said. 'And can we offer you a drink?'

'That would be kind of you.' She understood what constituted good manners.

'What would you like?'

'Coñac with just ice, please.'

'Ivor, would you like to pour the inspector a brandy, with ice, and me a sherry.'

'At once, my love.' He stood. 'One brandy, one sherry, and for me? A glass of Krug, a measure of Hine's V.S.O.P.? That's very special old pale, inspector.'

'It is kind of you to translate.'

'One can never know enough. A thirst for knowledge is the elixir of wisdom. The man who said that obviously wasn't from this island.'

'Would you get the drinks, Ivor,' she said.

'On my skates.' He left the room.

'I hope . . .'

He said nothing.

'You musn't think . . .'

Unwilling from a sense of loyalty to apologise for her husband's manner? He spoke quickly, hoping to disperse any embarrassment she might suffer. 'You haven't lived on the island for very long, señora?'

'Is that so very obvious?'

'Only because I understood from your husband that you would remain in this house until you found somewhere you like. Where would you hope that to be?'

'Anywhere but in a town. There's . . . there's so much noise. Late at night, people in the road shout at each other; mobylettes with the exhausts removed make a hideous racket. I've never been a sound sleeper and now I spend much of the night awake despite the earplugs I always wear at night. A friend suggested air-conditioning in order to be able to keep the windows shut but—'

Her husband interrupted her as he hurried into the room. 'You never got the brandy this morning.'

'It wasn't on the shopping list.'

'Yes it was. I wrote it down.'

Alvarez said, 'Señor, I should be very happy with a San Miguel.'

'Couldn't think of offering that, old man, much too plebian. There's a place just around the corner, so you won't be kept from sustenance for long, provided the place isn't filled with jabbering women careless of anyone else.' He left.

'Señora,' Alvarez said, as the front door was shut, 'I have to ask you a few questions and the absence of your husband makes that easier, but he may not be away for long which makes it necessary for me to speak more bluntly than I would wish. There is the possibility Señor Picare's death was not an accident. I need to understand, as far as that is possible, what kind of a man he was, so I am asking those who knew him what they can tell me.'

It was some time before she said, 'A friend rang up to tell

us the rumour that was going around. She said it was probably suicide.'

'It was not.'

'If it wasn't an accident . . . You're saying he may have been deliberately killed?'

'That is what we must determine and why I am talking to señoras who visited his home.'

'I went there from time to time so you think I may know what really happened?'

'No, señora. But you may know something which will enable me to discover that. Did you go there on several occasions?'

'Roughly, once a month.'

'You were friendly with him?'

She spoke forcefully. 'If you want the truth, I thought him contemptible. That surprises you?'

'I must admit to some extent, señora.'

'Who told you I visited him? One of the staff?'

'Yes.'

'Who thought, as you seem to, that that means I joined his harem? Let me get one thing straight. When I married, it was for ever, despite all difficulties, however antique that seems today. You think he would have bothered me, a forty-two-year-old with nothing to single me out from other women unless my morals were on a par with his? I went there to try to make him honour his promise to pay a reasonable sum each month towards the upkeep of the small, local sanctuary which cares for injured and stray dogs and cats about which no one else bothers.'

'The sanctuary is where?'

'Almost on the Llueso boundary in the direction of Inca. When I first came here, one so frequently saw cats and dogs by the side of the road, injured, dying. The sight so distressed me, I started the sanctuary and found local people willing to give time to help or money to pay the costs. Neil, when asked, immediately said he'd pay a generous monthly contribution.

'I hope I'm not being too catty to describe his act as the great man showing the public how generous he was. That didn't matter, his money was good, until the financial hurricane swept over the country. He stopped paying; I suspect not because he had to, as did so many others. The sanctuary's finances became critical, so I swallowed my pride, told him we would like to rename it the Picare Refuge and suggested the local English weekly paper would praise his generosity. It took several visits and much verbal boot-licking before he finally agreed to renew payments and for a larger amount. The sanctuary was saved.'

'Señora, will you accept my admiration?'

She smiled, providing her face with a measure of charm. 'I'd prefer a contribution.'

'You will have one. Sadly, I have to ask more questions.'

'Fire away.'

'Does your husband object to all the work you do for the refuge?'

'To some extent. It uses up so much of my time.'

'There is no other reason?'

'Are you still wondering, as I'm sure you were, whether the attraction was him, not what he could do for the sanctuary? I can best answer you by saying that had the cost of maintaining the refuge been my sleeping with him, I could not have brought myself to pay it.'

'Then your husband had no reason to hate Señor Picare.'

'Had he had, he would never have considered taking a single step to express his hatred. His character . . .' She hesitated, then spoke in a rush of words. 'It's so weak. It's not his fault. His mother never wanted children and blamed him for all the changes in her life. His father seldom spoke to him. When I met him, he was so shy and self-conscious that . . .'

Alvarez waited, then said, 'You knew you could provide him with a strong refuge from the world.'

'I suppose you could put it like that. But . . . but I loved him and still do.'

Because he allowed her to provide the strength which he needed. 'I have to ask you this. Did your husband fear that your explanation of your visits to Vista Bonita was no more than an attempt to disguise the fact you were having an affair with the señor?'

'If he'd believed that, his only thought would have been how to gain from the relationship.'

The front door opened, was shut with unnecessary force. Crane entered the room and held up a bottle. 'In honour of our visitor, the best brandy on their shelves.'

Alvarez recognised the label. Cheap and not on many shelves.

TWELVE

'Señor,' Alvarez said over the phone, 'we can strike out Ivor Crane from the list of possibles.'

'There is reason or are you relying on instinct despite its proven failures on several previous occasions?'

'He can best be called a complete twit.'

'You find yourself unable to offer a more informative description?'

'All bluster. Tried to make out he and his wife only lived in a pokey Mestara house until they found a bigger property. Obviously, they couldn't afford to live anywhere else. Then he served a coñac which could only be described as the dregs.'

'The taste is immaterial. What is of concern is that you were drinking when on duty. Something only very recently you have assured me you would never do.'

'He offered me a drink and I naturally refused, señor. He continued to try to persuade me to have one and it became obvious that, being English, he had that strange reluctance to drink on his own. Not wishing to increase his embarrassment, I finally accepted.'

'Why should he suffer any embarrassment from your refusal?'

'It could seem to him that I had judged him to be so hard up that his offer had been made only to conform with tradition.'

'Your avowed sympathy for his feelings became too strong?'

'He continued to press me and finally brought a bottle of coñac in to the room. In the circumstances, I decided that to continue to refuse would increase his embarrassment and that would cause resentment on his part. As you have said many times, when questioning someone, take every opportunity to keep him at ease.'

'In my authority, I listen to many excuses. Some are acceptable, some are possessed of a grain of truth, most are sufficiently unbelievable to question the speaker's intelligence. You have just shown you denigrate my intelligence.'

'I have never had the slightest reason to do such a thing, señor.'

'It can be said to be both our misfortunes that I cannot return the denial. I have yet to learn why you consider Crane incapable of causing Picare's death.'

'His character. His wife scorns him, much of what he says is an attempt to make out he's sharp and successful when it is obvious he is weak and a failure. If Picare was dragged under the water in his pool, the person concerned must have a strong character. Crane's wife suggested he could never do anything which would put him within a hundred metres of danger.'

'You did not consider she might have been lying?'

'Señor, she scorns him.'

'Her emotion was not an act?'

'Because of the tone with which she spoke, because in the short time during which I was there, I understood she had every reason to scorn him.'

'For the moment, it is necessary to rely on your judgment. Your report of Giselle Dunkling?'

'I have not spoken to her yet.'

'The Lynette woman?'

'I have not had the time to question her. I have been working day and night—'

The line became dead.

He looked at his wristwatch. Questioning a possible suspect should not be rushed so he would speak to one or both of the other women the following morning.

He left the post and was walking across the old square when a woman said, 'Hullo'. He came to a stop, half turned. The face was familiar.

'You look very busy, inspector.' Carolina Pellisa, the daily at Vista Bonita.

'I am having to work harder than ever.'

'Do you know yet what . . . what happened?'

'I still have to make certain.'

'Then maybe . . .' She looked away.

'You have something to tell me?'

She looked back at him. 'I think so, but . . .'

'I should like to hear what it is. Let's find somewhere to sit. Club Llueso is just over there. You might like a coffee?'

'I should, but if I have one I'll be late at work.'

'You go by bus?'

'There isn't one which would get me there on time, so I cycle.'

'Up that mountain?'

She smiled. 'I call it a hill, so it's easier and the exercise is good for me.'

That was a general misconception. 'Tell them you've been delayed by a puncture. Better still, that I stopped you and asked questions.'

'I'd rather not. I don't want Rosalía to know. She says we mustn't talk about what happened because that could become disloyal to them who pay our wages.'

An unusual attitude in this day and age. 'Very well, no coffee. But we can't talk here with tourists everywhere. We'll go to the post.'

'Oh!'

'You'd rather not?'

'I was just thinking . . . Anyone who knows me might think I was in trouble.' She paused briefly. 'It'll give them something to talk about!'

They left the square, walked the short distance to the post. He said they had to go upstairs and she went first, had to wait for him to join her. He showed her into his room and set a chair by the side of the desk.

'What do you want to tell me, Carolina?'

'I don't want to, it's just I think I should.'

'Because you understand the duty of everyone. I'm afraid you must tell me what you know. Does it concern the late señor?'

'No.'

'Then who?'

'She becomes so upset over so many things, even meaningless ones. Rosalía who is fond of her, noticed she'd become so concerned, she was afraid Marta would worry herself ill. She talked to Marta for a long time to try to find out what was wrong and eventually learned Marta was terrified she'd be arrested and imprisoned.'

'What on earth could make her think that possible?'

'You questioned her after the señor died.'

'I had to, much as I disliked doing so.'

'She told you she heard the visitor say goodbye to the señor when he was by the pool and then the visitor drove away.'

'That's correct.'

'After speaking to you, she began to worry she was wrong.'

'In what respect?'

'Because she heard the visitor say goodbye, she expected him to leave immediately. But now she thinks maybe she got it wrong and perhaps she finished the work she was doing before she heard the car leave.'

'How long would it have taken her to finish the work?'

'I can't say.'

'What changed her mind?'

'She's been so disturbed since the señor died, Rosalía wonders if she's making up the mistake in some way to lessen her sense of shame.'

'Shame over what?'

'Perhaps thinking the señor would ever marry her. I don't know. I can only tell you what Rosalía suggested.'

'What do you think?'

'As I've said, I don't have an opinion. I'm just a country person, but I've learned not to try to judge what other people will do and think.'

'Then you have learned more than most. What you've told me means I must have another word with Marta.'

'If you do, she'll tell Rosalía who'll know I must have spoken to you about this. She'll be so annoyed, she might advise the señora to get rid of me because of my malicious gossip. What I earn here is important because everything has become so expensive and with so many people out of work, I would have terrible trouble trying to find another job.'

'I'll make certain Rosalía does not know you have spoken to me.'

She hesitated, seemed about to repeat her request, then stood. He accompanied her down to the front door. It was almost *merienda* time, so he walked across to Club Llueso.

*   *   *

'Given up work for the day?' Roca asked.

'Taking a breather to rest the brain.'

'It's still active?'

'I'll have a café cortado and a coñac.'

'You do know you can have coffee on its own?'

Alvarez sat at a window table, considered what he had heard, not the people passing outside, a couple of whom were dressed in skirts so short he would normally have noticed them. Since there was no reason to believe Marta had had reason to lie to Rosalía, her later evidence concerning Russell could seem to be acceptable. Yet if her original evidence had been fallacious, had she recovered sufficiently for her altered evidence to be accurate?

Roca brought coffee and coñac to the table. Having put them down, he waited. Alvarez looked up. 'Something bothering you?'

'Wondering if you've anything to say.'

'Such as?'

'Thank you.'

'Do I expect to be thanked when all I've done is the job I'm paid to do?'

'How would you know when you don't do it?' Roca returned behind the bar.

Alvarez drank some of the brandy, poured the remainder into the coffee. When Salas had named Russell to be the likely murderer, if there had been a murder, he had questioned whether a man would murder for the sake of a legacy, generous but not a fortune. That question remained. So did the logical answer – very probably not. But human nature was often governed by emotion rather than logic.

Did he speak to Marta or Rosalía first? Salas had demanded he questioned Russell again, so perhaps the answer was determined. It was satisfying to sort out a problem even when the answer called for more work. He signalled to Roca to bring another coñac. He began to notice the public. A young woman wore a skirt so short that modesty could not be in her vocabulary.

'Get your eye-balls back in before they fall out,' Roca said, as he put a filled glass of brandy on the table

THIRTEEN

'Señor Russell is maybe on the beach,' the receptionist at Hotel Tamit said.

'You've seen him leave?' Alvarez asked.

'No.'

He could not understand why someone should willingly grill himself. The sun was not there to provide the pain of sunburn, but the pleasure of sitting under a shade umbrella while having a drink. 'Then would you use the PA system to make certain he isn't still in the hotel.'

'It's probably not working.'

'Give it a try.'

The receptionist, with ill grace, swivelled round on his chair and depressed one switch of the ancient apparatus on a shelf behind the desk. He spoke into the microphone and was clearly annoyed when his suggestion of failure was proved wrong as a nearby speaker on the inner wall relayed, in tortured tones, the request for Señor Russell to come to reception.

Russell walked out of the bar, came to a sudden stop when he saw Alvarez; uneasily, he shifted his weight from one leg to the other before he crossed over. Alvarez greeted him.

'Hullo, inspector,' he said uneasily.

'I won't bother you for long, just need a brief word or two.'

The lift doors had opened and a blonde (unlikely genuine), hurried across to where they stood. 'I heard you being called. Is something up?' She studied Alvarez.

'No need to call for the fire engine. Just met a friend and we need a chat. Go on into the bar and I'll be with you in no time.'

She said, in little-girl tones, 'I've been told never to drink on my own until I'm twenty-one.'

Alvarez tried to work out how long ago that ban had been imposed.

'Order a champagne cocktail and tell them it's on my account.' Russell said.

'If you take too long, I'll become thirsty.' She went into the bar.

A frequent complaint? he wondered. 'I need a word so can you suggest somewhere quiet where we can go?'

'Not really.'

'We'll try the lounge. Doesn't look inviting enough to be overcrowded.'

They sat in the otherwise deserted lounge. A waiter took their orders. Russell's evident worry increased as Alvarez kept the conversation neutral.

The waiter returned, put a lager and a brandy down, spiked the bill. Alvarez drank, replaced the glass on the table. 'You'll know why I'm here, of course.'

'I've said all I possibly can.'

'Then you won't keep the young lady in solitude for long. I imagine you haven't received your legacy yet?'

'That sort of thing takes for ever.'

'I don't suppose this hotel costs you much, but experience suggests your companion will expect to be treated generously.'

'I saved to come out here and chose this hotel because it's cheap and looked much better on the travel agent's brochure. I can just afford a little entertainment.'

'Why did you come to the island?'

'I needed a break; by reputation it's a whole lot quieter than Ibiza.'

'And you're not an all-night reveller. But more to the point, was it because Señor Picare lived here?'

'No.'

'You had a meal at Vista Bonita on the first night of your arrival.'

'Who says I did?'

'Perhaps you were in a hurry to ask Señor Picare for money.'

'Certainly not. Even if that were true, what of it? We're related and he had a lot more than he knew what to do with. Why shouldn't he share some of it?'

'A political question, so I am not equipped to answer. Why have you lied to me?'

'I haven't.'

'Not when you mentioned how glad Señor Picare was to see you; how much he enjoyed talking about old times.'

'He did.'

'A lie can be given by silence as well as by words. You told me he was by the pool when you said goodbye to each other; you walked to your car and drove off. If that were true, he was still alive when you left and you could have no responsibility for his death.'

'That's what happened.'

'Is it?'

'He asked me to come again and have another meal and what would I like.'

'Just prior to your departure, there was no such invitation.'

'Who says?'

'One of the staff.'

'Whoever it was is lying.'

'Why should she?'

'How the hell do I know?'

'Señor Picare's bank statements show he drew a fairly large sum the day after you arrived on the island. Did he give you money?'

'No.'

'As I have learned, he was far from generous unless he gained a benefit from being so.' It was time for another gamble. 'I have spoken to the cashier who cashed his cheque. He remembers that the man who handed him a cheque signed by the señor had red hair and the white skin of someone who was only recently on the island. There can be little doubt the cashier will be able to identify the person concerned. I will ask again, was it you?'

Russell picked up his glass and drained it. 'Look, I'm not a fool. When I heard about Neil's death and you questioned me, I understood I was the last person to see him and if you people knew he had given me some money, it must seem I had something to do with what happened.'

'Conclusions can be correct as well as obvious.'

'I didn't . . . couldn't . . .' He picked up his glass and went do drink, found it empty.

Alvarez signalled to a waiter.

Their fresh drinks in front of them, he said, 'Tell me about your last visit to Vista Bonita.'

His hand shaking sufficiently to ripple the level of the whisky he had chosen, Russell raised the glass and drank. 'When we'd had liqueurs, he said he was going for a swim and I should join him. I told him, one shouldn't go into water within an hour of eating. He laughed at me. It was an old wives' tale, but if I liked to believe it . . . He said he might be seeing me again, I left. I swear to God, that's true. I don't know what happened afterwards, I wasn't there when he drowned because he scorned the old precept.'

'Was the luncheon delicious?'

The unexpected question momentarily bewildered Russell.

'You can't remember what you ate?'

'I didn't like it.'

'Why's that? Rosalía was not well?'

'Who?'

'The cook. A magician in the kitchen.'

'Neil said she was good and the dish was one of his favourites. But I don't like pork, especially when it's got something on it and is wrapped in cabbage leaves. I left almost half and that seemed to annoy him.'

With good reason. *Lomo con col*. A favourite Mallorquin dish; when cooked by Rosalía, it would have been memorable. 'What was the sweet?'

'He said that was another of his favourites – vanilla ice cream with maple syrup. I hardly had any because ice cream always makes my teeth jump.'

'For you, an unfortunate meal. What did you do after it?'

'Went out to the pool patio and had coffee and liqueurs.'

'What did you choose?'

'Didn't have any choice. He liked green Chartreuse, so that's what I had to have. Burned my tongue.'

'A meal made ever more unfortunate. Having suffered, what was your next disaster?'

'As I said to you already, he said he was going for a swim and I should join him.'

'Which you did?'

'Again, as I told you already, it was too soon after we'd

eaten. He laughed and said that was a myth. It happens to be one I believe. So, I thanked him for the meal, said goodbye and left.'

'Where was he when you said goodbye?'

'I don't know. I'm getting confused with all the questions.'

'He was by the pool shortly before you drove away. Would you agree?'

'How can I, when I can't remember clearly?'

'It would save complications if you could. Unfortunately, I must return to work. Incidentally, I hope you are not thinking of leaving the island in the near future.'

'How can I when you've got my passport?'

'With money and the right contact, it would not be difficult to buy another. Alternately, you might tell the British Consul your passport has been stolen and would he issue you with a replacement.'

'When you'll have made certain he knows mine had been legally taken from me, not lost.'

'You have experience in such problems?'

FOURTEEN

'Señor . . .' Alvarez suddenly stopped mid-flow to put down the receiver and reach across the desk to pick up the burning cigarette which had fallen from the ashtray on to some paper.

'What is it?'

Salas had spoken sufficiently sharply for Alvarez to guess what had been said even though the receiver still lay on the desk. He hurriedly picked it up. 'I'm sorry, I had to retrieve the notes I made on my interview.'

'They should have been ready before you began to phone.'

'Señor Russell has admitted he went to Vista Bonita on the day Señor Picare drowned and it is clear that he did so in order to ask for money. He was invited to lunch. Although the meal would have been delicious – as you will know, *Lomo con Col* cooked well is a revelation when the meat is tender and the cabbage leaves are neither too crisp or sloppy—'

'I find it difficult to decide whether you are more interested in food or, regrettably, matters of a sexual nature. I am interested in neither. Why was he asked to lunch?'

'He is, I understand, some vague relation. Also, the señora was out for the day and it must have been pleasant for Picare to have someone new to talk to. After the meal, the señor said he was going for a swim and Russell should join him. Russell did not because he believed it dangerous to swim too soon after a meal.'

'Quite correct.'

'I believe that proposition is now largely held to be incorrect.'

'You speak with medical knowledge?'

'No, señor.'

'Repeating a comment then from some ill-informed person.'

'Russell thanked the señor for the meal when they were by the pool, drove away. This contradicts Marta's evidence.

It becomes necessary to decide who is the more likely to be remembering accurately or, perhaps, lying.'

'Your judgment?'

'Marta is correct.'

'Your reason?'

'She has nothing to gain whether believed or disbelieved; on the contrary, Russell has much to lose if disbelieved. I have shown that Marta was unlikely to have heard what was said by the pool.'

'Do I correctly understand your suggestion of how events proceeded? Russell undressed, got into the pool, suddenly and violently dragged Señor Picare underwater, made certain he was dead, left the pool, quickly dried, rapidly dressed, drove away. Why does Marta say she could hear what they said when your judgment is that she could not.'

'It would be incorrect to say her mind has flown—'

'It would be absurd. Can you not describe what you believe the state of her mind to have been in intelligent terms?'

'There is no reason to accept that what she says is totally wrong. Had she detailed a longer and more involved conversation, I would wonder is she was making out she had heard more than she did.'

'Why would she?'

'She knows, or guesses, her information is very important. Because she is something of a lost soul . . .'

'You are reporting to your commanding officer, not writing a novel for love-sick maidens.'

'She may be using imagination to gain our attention.'

'Very unlikely. Question her again.'

'Her mother may well not allow that.'

'You will demand to speak to her.'

'And when the mother complains to the media, tells them the cuerpo has reverted to the past and ignores the rights of those who live in a democracy and condemns without justification?'

'Your imagination surpasses imagination. Do you intend to arrest Russell?'

'Not on the strength of such evidence as we have. Looking at it from your point of view, señor, what if it is finally decided no progress could have been made because Señor Picare's death was an accident? To dismiss an officer from his case because he fails to solve a crime which was not committed might be considered over-reacting.'

'Have you yet questioned Giselle Dunkling, the Lynette woman and Debra Crane?'

'Not all of them, señor. I would have done had you not demanded that I re-question Russell.'

'When you are called to Hades, Alvarez, will you seek dismissal on the grounds that all your sins were the faults of others?'

He had assumed he would be able to find the address in the telephone book. He turned to the Llueso section, looked down the As without success. If she had a residencia, he could ask Palma to name the address, but those who worked in that office always resented being asked to do anything. Perhaps Rosalía could help.

Marta opened the front door of Vista Bonita. He asked how she was.

'All right,' was her only answer. From her apparent tense-ness, the way she looked at him, away, at him again, he guessed she wanted to say something. He stepped inside, said quietly. 'Is something bothering you, Marta?'

She looked around the hall, making certain she could not be overheard, yet remained silent.

'Where is the señora?' he asked.

'Upstairs. She's not well and can hardly eat anything.'

'Then let's invite ourselves into the staff sitting room.'

'But if she wants me . . .'

'Rosalía will find out why.'

She reluctantly followed him into the small room. He shut the door, took a pace towards a chair when the door was flung back. Rosalía entered. 'What's going on? Why have you brought her in here?' she demanded.

'To have a word with her.'

'On your own?'

'Naturally.'

'A word?'

The idea was so absurd that he did not immediately understand the reason for her angry concern. When he did, he said,
'You can think that?'

'Easily.'

'Then you need help. She wants to talk to me.'

She spoke to Marta. 'If you need help, call out.' She left.

'What does she mean?' Marta asked. 'Why should I need
help?'

'I doubt she understands any more than I do.'

'You're angry. Because of me?'

'I couldn't sleep last night and that always makes me sound
grouchy.'

'I can't sleep since . . .' She stopped.

'Have a word with your doctor and see if he can help.'

'Perhaps yours could help you.'

'I will ask him. Marta, when we were in the hall, it seemed
you wanted to tell me something. Did you?'

She looked down at the floor.

'If you're troubled, tell me why and I will do my very best
to help you.'

'Do you . . . Do you still think . . . that it was my fault—'

He interrupted her halting question. 'I have never believed
that you were in any way implicated in the señor's death. He
knew no shame over his behaviour towards you, so he was
not overcome by remorse and committed suicide.' She needed
reason to accept his words. 'We now believe he may have
been killed.'

'No!'

She failed to understand that he was removing any sense
of guilt from her. 'Someone may have murdered him.'

'I . . . I've been so desperately worried.'

'Without any cause.'

'Do you really mean that?'

'As if I had said it under oath.'

'Then, I can stop thinking . . .?' She darted forward and
lightly kissed him on the cheek, hurried out of the room.

The pleasure gained from the reassurance he had provided
her was swept away by imaginative, unwanted possibilities.
What if they never identified someone with both the motive

and the guilt so that suicide seemed the inevitable conclusion. How would Marta react to his false assurance? A lie often had poisonous tentacles.

He returned into the hall, walked across to the kitchen. Rosalía was seated at the table, drinking coffee.

'You behaved like a bitch.' he said roughly.

'You'll be used to that.'

'How could you think I'd behave towards her as Picare did?'

'Perhaps I was a bit hasty' she admitted. 'But I've been so worried about her becoming desperately depressed because she thinks she was responsible. Don't you understand? I find the two of you in there with the door shut. D'you expect me to shrug my shoulders and walk on?'

'To find out the truth before shouting at me for being a pervert.'

'Really, you aren't all that dissimilar from the señor. Your pleasures are mostly the same as his.'

'Like hell they are!'

'He was after any women who looked sweetly eager, you always show the same interest. His loyalty to his marriage is matched by yours to a virtuous bachelorhood. Now, would you like some coffee with the scent of coñac?'

'Laced with arsenic?'

'Only if no one can find out I gave it to you.'

He sat. She poured out coffee and added a solid dash of brandy to each cup, carried cups and saucers to the table, sat opposite to him.

He drank, appreciated the proportion of coñac to coffee. 'Tell me something, Rosalía.'

'The answer remains, 'No.'

'I want you to help me.'

'To do what?'

'Señor Russell told me a woman named Lynette came here frequently. Did you ever come across her?'

'Yes. Lynette Arcton.'

'Do you know where she lives?'

'Stony cottage – English countryside romanticism.'

'Do you know where that is?'

'On the first road below Puig Grog, in the urbanizacion.'

'And do you know anything about a Giselle Dunkling?'

'She is a physiotherapist and came here to help the señor's back, but you make out she was having an affair with him.'

'I did not. Your mind raced to that conclusion. Do you know anything more about her?'

'No more than most, but it seems perhaps more than you.'

'Why? What are you getting at?'

'She partakes in a ménage à trois. There are three of them who live together and they claim that one is her half-brother, however I can assure you he is not. His introduction to society was to stem the opinion of those who feel it necessary to be outraged by others' lives.'

'How did you learn about the relationship?'

'Why didn't you know until I told you?'

He stared at nothing, his mind trying to assess the consequences of what she had said. Two men sharing one woman was a situation unlikely to lead to domestic unity. One of the two men was bound to feel short-changed.

'You look as if you have no experience of such relationships,' she said.

'True.'

'And I've been thinking of you as a man of the world. Perhaps your air of confidence is a shield to hide uncertainty and nervousness? Would you like to finish your coffee and leave because I have to prepare lunch for the señora who now wishes to eat.'

'She has become reconciled to the death of the señor?'

'You judge by the time it would take you to overcome grief at your wife's death?'

He stood, walked to the doorway, stopped. 'What's the menu?'

'Fillets of turbot.'

'The same pleasure for you?'

'Being on my own.'

He walked up to the rock-built house, modern to judge from the number of windows and their sizes. The front door was panelled and oiled. He sounded the bell.

A woman opened the door. 'Yes?'

'Señora Arcton? I am Inspector Alvarez. I should be grateful if I might speak to you.'

'Because of Neil?'

'That is so.'

'You'd better come in.'

The entrada was barely furnished. She was of an appearance that wasn't obviously eye-catching. A woman might criticise her – too large a mouth, long neck, poor hair style, make-up too generous – but a man would note the indications of a passionate nature.

In the sitting room was a display cabinet in which were several model World War II aircraft. He recognised a Spitfire, a Me 109, and a Lancaster; others had familiar shapes, but he could not name them.

She noticed his interest. 'My grandfather was in the RAF. He made them.'

'They are wonderfully well done, señora.'

'He could make wood and metal do as he wanted.'

'In my hands a piece of wood becomes splinters.'

She smiled.

Her dark brown hair was generously fashioned, her eyes were possessed of a depth of blue which engaged poets, her nose could have been modelled by an artist. 'Señora, I believe you knew Señor Picare?'

'That's correct.'

'Would you refer to him as a close friend?'

'How close is that?'

'You frequently visited him at Vista Bonita.'

'How frequent is frequent?'

'Perhaps it will make things easier if I explain that I am trying to find out as much about the señor's life as possible.'

'Then it is not just a rumour that it may not have been an accident?'

'I will be frank. We still cannot be certain whether or not his unfortunate death was accidental. As a consequence, we are speaking to those who knew him in order to learn if he suffered from depression or a mental illness, was known to have argued bitterly with others, expressed a fear of someone, hinted he might be in danger.'

'He argued, but when I heard him, it was never angrily. I imagine he annoyed many people.'

'Why do you think that?'

'If the tittle-tattle is correct, he was a small-time farmer who sold land for development which enabled him able to retire wealthy. There are still two or three wives of retired higher-ranking officers in the armed forces who are living on reduced circumstances because of inflation and increased taxation; they refer to him as the jumped-up cowman. Naturally, their contempt doesn't prevent their attending his parties and enjoying the fruits of his unearned success.'

'You sound as if your resentment was for their attitude?'

'Cynical amusement rather than resentment.'

'You are unwilling to say how frequently you went to Vista Bonita?'

'Too difficult to remember.'

'Was Señora Picare happy to meet you.'

'Happiness seems to have escaped her a long time ago.'

'Was she always at Vista Bonita when you were?'

'Seldom. Inspector, would you like a drink? If so, what would you choose?'

'Thank you. May I have a coñac with just ice?'

She stood. 'I won't be a moment.'

After she left, he studied the three framed photographs on the top shelf of the simple bookcase, filled with hardcover and paperback books. In each photograph she was with the same smiling man.

She returned, handed him a glass, sat. 'Salud, inspector.'

It was a pleasant coñac, not far short of a good one. He held the glass in his hand, enjoying the coolness of the glass. 'I asked you if Señora Picare was always there when you visited Vista Bonita and I think you said not. Is that correct?'

'Yes.'

'Was she ever there?'

'I don't remember her being so.'

'Perhaps you made certain she would not be?'

'You need me to answer?'

'It's just that . . .' He stopped.

'People are even more hypocritical over sex than wealth.

Inspector, my marriage was happy and fun and when I remember Sam it's like rejoining a dream. Sam was a "let's do it now because tomorrow we may not be able to" person. He had a good income, spent more. When he died, bank accounts were overdrawn, payments on the mortgage were in arrears, creditors became very noisy. By the time things were sorted out, his estate was virtually nil. I had some savings, but they were well short of comfortable. I came out here and rented a flat, knowing it was stupid because I would return to England virtually penniless. But I had to find a way to accept Sam's death and was certain the change in surroundings might help to do that.'

She looked across. 'Your glass is empty. May I refill it?'

'Thank you.'

They both stood, she to take his glass, he to hand it to her. Her brief expression of surprise indicated she had expected him, as a Mallorquin, to remain seated whilst she fetched and carried. Seen close to, her ear lobes were unusually large. An indication of emotional vulnerability. He returned to his seat, she carried out the glasses, soon returned with them refilled.

Having handed him his glass, she walked over to the window and stared out. 'I fell in love with the port, the background, the beautiful bay, never more so than when occasionally there is a sea fret and the far mountains pierce it. I believe it's hell to do business with anyone here, but it did the trick for me. I became at peace, never forgetting him, but no longer cursing the young driver of the other car which skidded because of speed. Sam was gone, but he had given me times to be treasured.' She drank, put the glass down, stared into space.

Her thoughts must have been similar to his when Juana María had died. Why had it happened to her? Why had she not checked the last step so that the car missed her? Why did God suffer drunken drivers rather than the innocent?

Lynette Arcton resumed speaking. 'I had to wake up in the real world and understand my life was going to have to be pretty basic. No more treats to relieve a bad day, wine at meals, a drink or two in the evening. I was faced with the problem all ex-pats do when they consider returning home. Where would I live? Property here has become difficult to sell and its value has fallen more than the equivalent would have in England. How would I gain a mortgage when one has to put down an ever-larger deposit, I was a widow, had none of the skills needed to get a well-paid job?

'People were kind after Sam's death; they provided company when I needed it, invited me to their parties. At one, I met Neil. That he was there was a surprise since it was not a flashy party; that he didn't just nod the introduction and dismiss me from his mind surprised me even more. He chose to sit next to me for the meal and afterwards quietly, sympathetically asked me how I was getting on.

'I may have had a little too much to drink because it was one of my down days and I needed soft useless sympathy. I told him I was going to have to return home, how I dreaded the coming weather, isolation, and indifference of others. He asked me why I had decided to return. Normally, I'd have given a neutral answer, but I told him why. He sympathised and said I'd be sure to find a way to stay on the island. A traditional assurance, meant to soothe, but always irritating.

'The next Tuesday, he called at my place, handed me a sealed envelope, said he couldn't stay but hoped we'd meet again soon. In the envelope was a receipt for my overdue mortgage repayment. Soon afterwards, he said he hoped I'd go with him to the newly-opened restaurant in Soller. I wanted to know why he'd paid the mortgage debt. He said he gained more pleasure from using his money to help people than anything he could buy. Not being naive, I decided I'd rather eat here, on my own.

'He again asked me out to lunch and named that restaurant in Soller. Someone had told me she'd eaten there and the meal had been superb. I always find it difficult to refuse champagne. We had a great meal, he drove me back here, hoped I'd enjoyed the break and left. He asked me out a couple more times, for dinner. The routine each time was the same, a delicious meal, amusing talk, a cheek-kiss goodbye.

'It's easy to say what happened next, difficult to explain. He asked me to dinner at Vista Bonita; his cook was a culinary genius, the meal would be better than we could have at any restaurant. We ate, drank, ended up in bed, despite all Frank's warnings.' She looked quickly at him. 'And now you're thinking my marriage couldn't have been so perfect when I didn't bother about dishonouring it.'

'Death draws an impenetrable line.'

'Many ex-pats would disagree.'

'I often disagree with their values.'

'You may dislike me for saying this, but you're a very unusual policeman.'

'I accept that as a compliment.'

'You don't resemble Sam in any particular way, yet you make me think of him.'

A comparison of great worth. 'Señora, I hope I have not distressed you?'

'You may even have helped.'

'I hope that proves to be so.' He stood. 'I must leave.'

'Before another drink?'

As he drove away, he remembered Juana-María with greater clarity than usual. It was as if another's acceptance of death had increased his sense of loss.

FIFTEEN

'I have questioned Señora Arcton, señor,' Alvarez said, receiver to his ear.

'To what effect?' Salas asked.

'She admits she had an affair with Señor Picare, however unlikely.'

'I am surprised you consider any relationship unlikely.'

'She is not beautiful and he usually chose those who were more obviously attractive. I think it's the señora's qualities which attracted him.'

'Perhaps it was her readiness to forget she had been married that attracted him?'

'Her compassion, sympathy, understanding—'

'Complete your report without searching for emotions which could not more contradict the facts.'

'It's not that straightforward. She suffered financial troubles and could not meet her mortgage repayments so was in danger of having her flat repossessed. Picare never said what he was going to do, but one day handed her a receipt for the overdue mortgage repayment. When she asked him why he had done that, he said he liked to use his money to help people.'

'Nothing could be more straightforward. She well understood his motive and behaved like a puta.'

'Never.'

'What name do you use to describe a woman who sells her body?'

'A puta sells herself to anyone who'll pay.'

'The number of customers is immaterial, the relationship between action and money is. She related her financial problems in order to engage his interest in what she had to offer.'

'Señor, she attracted his interested sympathy without artifice. If you question her, you will discover her captivating character.'

'You suggest I meet this woman in order to judge her to be of the nature you contend rather than the one she clearly is?'

'I think you would find—'

'I have no intention of searching. Did you gain any information from her which could be termed material?'

'She knows someone and he advised her against a friendship with Señor Picare. That might have been a quiet warning or a product of jealousy.'

'I will not waste time asking you for your judgment, whether you have yet questioned this man or if you know his name.'

'Frank.'

'Frank who?'

'I've only heard the señora refer to him by his Christian name.'

'And you did not think to demand his surname and address?'

'I very much doubt she will accept a demand. She will only give me the details if persuaded.'

'Persuade her.'

'It might be better if someone else did that.'

'Why?'

'It could be called a conflict of interests.'

'You are making even less sense than usual. You will question Frank to discover if he suffers from an amoral jealousy sufficient to consider him a suspect.'

'Señor . . .'

'Is Señora Dunkling of greater respectability?'

'That, I suppose, depends on one's point of view.'

'Are you incapable of giving a straight answer?'

'Señora Dunkling enjoys a ménage à trois.'

'What!'

'It is a situation in which a woman lives with two men or a man with—'

'To my regret, I am aware of what the description means. My exclamation was expressing surprised shock that such immoral conduct should occur on this island.'

'It is fairly common elsewhere.'

'You have reason other than desire to make such assertion?'

'I'll question the two men to find out if there is a question of jealousy. That's possible because one man might have exceeded his allowance.'

There was a silence.

'Alvarez, it is very probable it would be an advantage for this investigation to be placed in other hands. However, I do not wish it to be widely known that such immorality exists in my area. You will question the husband.'

'And the co-husband?'

'You succeed in making a simple word sound offensive.'

The lift stopped, the door opened, Alvarez walked over to the door of the flat, rang the bell. This was opened by a woman of generous build who wore blouse and slacks. She regarded him with the hint of hostility Mallorquins often showed an unidentified visitor.

'Are Señor and Señora Dunkling here?' he asked in Mallorquin.

'I can't say.'

A typically evasive answer. Her accent marked her as a fellow Lluesan. If women were allowed to take part in the Festival of the Moors and Christians, she would no doubt have wielded a broom handle with sufficient force to make one or two 'Moors' unhappy.

'I would like to speak to them.'

A man came into the hall. 'Who is it, Juana?' he asked in fractured Spanish.

Alvarez answered the question in English.

'What brings you here, inspector?'

'I have to investigate the unfortunate death of Señor Picare and you may be able to help me. You are Señor Dunkling?'

'I am.'

'May I enter?'

'Sorry. Do come in.'

The sitting room was crowded with bulky furniture. On each of the two tables were orchids in flower, held upright with wooden supports, in attractive ceramic bowls. There was a well-filled bookcase, an entertainment stand on which was a large TV and a DVD player, two heavily inlaid poufs, three armchairs and a settee. Another middle-aged man, also in shorts, T-shirt and sandals, sat on the settee; in one of the easy chairs was a woman whose upper contours of breasts were visible through the over-generous line of the neck of her frock.

'Inspector Alvarez,' Dunkling announced. 'My wife, Giselle, and brother-in-law, Turner' were introduced with a brief wave of the arm.

'I suppose you're here because of Neil?' Turner said.

'Yes, señor. I wish to learn what you can tell me about Señor Picare.'

Dunkling spoke first. 'There's very little we can say about him, inspector. We were invited to one or two of his parties, but that provided the few times we met.'

'You were not firm friends?'

'We lead a quiet life. Were that not from necessity, we might have been more favourably regarded.'

'Nevertheless, you met the señor from time to time?'

'Apart from the parties? In the village, perhaps, when it was a good morning, how are you and goodbye.'

'My understanding is that generally speaking, he was not well liked.'

'Money in the hands of someone who once had very little is regarded with suspicion since it is the reversal of a stable society.'

'Would you think anyone had a more definite reason for disliking him?'

'One imagines there must be husbands who do, unless they're enfeebled.'

'Perhaps a Spanish husband or boyfriend might have had reason to hate him?'

'Everything is possible, but I reckon he would have avoided becoming involved with a Spanish lady. The reputation of a Spanish husband is that he still regards his wife's virtue as his concern.'

'You have knowledge of any husband Señor Picare might have cuckolded?'

'"Cuckold". A description which has almost become extinct despite the increased times when it could be used. Inspector, we were due to meet a friend at Bar Imperial some time ago. He will expect us to be late, but not so late as to be rude. We have told you all we know, so would it be all right if we bring things to an end?'

'I shall want to have a word with the señora, but will return another time.'

'I'd rather get it over with,' she said.

'What can you tell him I haven't?' Dunkling asked her. 'And don't forget, Harry and Charles will be there.'

'You haven't mentioned that before. A good reason for staying here.'

'I'm damned if I know why you don't like Charles.'

'His hands have wandering instincts.'

'A compliment.'

'One I can happily forego.'

'Then stay here and I will tell Charles how sorry you are at not being able to meet.'

Dunkling stood. 'Don't let the inspector browbeat you.'

The two men left. A moment later, it sounded as if the door had been shut with considerable force. An expression of annoyance or uneasiness? Alvarez wondered.

'Señora—'

She interrupted him. 'There's really nothing to tell you.'

'Even though you frequently visited Vista Bonita?'

'Only from time to time.'

'Was it not more frequently?'

'No.'

'Like most staff, those who worked for Señor Picare are curious. They have told me you were often there.'

'If so, not for the reason you imagine.'

'I am not imagining anything.'

'Then you'll have been told Neil tried to jump every woman who came within his reach? I was never within a casual reach. I'm a physiotherapist.'

'You were exercising your professional skills?'

'Rather than my amatory ones. Neil has . . . had a painful back. In the past, I'd helped some ex-pats with their problems, he heard about this and asked me to treat him. I managed to relieve some of the pain and restore good mobility.'

'Did Señor Dunkling object to your treating him?'

'No.'

'He was not worried by Picare's reputation?'

'He is my husband.'

'I am trying to ascertain the exact nature of Señor Picare's death, so I must ask again, did the señor not object to your treating Señor Picare?'

'At first, he seemed worried, but that didn't last. It was Frank who made a bit of a fuss.'

'Frank?'

'Frank Macrone.'

'Why should he object when your husband so obviously trusted you?'

'He has the habit of leaping to the wrong conclusion, especially in matters which aren't his concern. I always think of him as living in a black and white, not a coloured world.'

'Did your husband ever suggest to him that he should not think ill of these visits?'

'In the course of a vigorous row which ended up by clearing the air.'

'Señora, I gained the impression that you and the señors were uneasy when you learned of my identity.'

She shrugged her shoulders. 'Can't comment except for myself. I wasn't going to laugh when a detective wanted a word.'

'You did not fear I was here because of something which did concern you?'

'When I knew I had done nothing to warrant the police's interest?'

There was a thump on the door and Turner entered. 'You OK?' he asked Giselle.

'As yet, there is no sign of the thumbscrews.'

Alvarez said, 'And will remain hidden, señor. Since I have learned all I need to know, I was about to thank Señora Dunkling and ask her to tell you I'd be grateful if you would come and have a word.'

She left. Alvarez suggested they sat. 'Señor, as I may have said, I wish to learn more about Señor Picare's life and how he was regarded by others. Did you like him?'

'A tricky question. I'd say, he interested me,' Turner replied.

'I have spoken to several other people and none of them seemed to have found him interesting.'

'We don't all live in the same world. He used his wealth as a magnet, was ostentatious, careless about the grief he caused. Most people have a dark side and hypocritically try to hide this from themselves as well as others. He didn't. That suggests a degree of courage.'

Or perverse pride, Alvarez thought to himself. 'Did you sometimes accompany Giselle when she went to Vista Bonita?'

'And show my trust was false or that Giselle's husband didn't trust her? The only time I've been there has been when we were invited to one of his parties and accepted for the same reason we condemn others – the chance briefly to enjoy luxury. But there was only that one time and since then we've had very little contact, especially as our friend Frank has reason to dislike him so much.'

'Why the dislike?'

'Neil tried to have a fling with Frank's wife. Why d'you want to know?'

'No specific reason, just the wish to learn all I can.'

'I doubt there was much contact between the two of them.'

'Do you know where Señor Macrone lives?'

'Ca'n Macrone, in Mitjorn.'

Another example of foreigners' egotism or ignorance in calling houses after their names rather than their nicknames.

'For the record, I doubt Frank knows any more about Neil's private life than I do. And I'd be grateful if this meeting could come to an end. I do have to go out.'

'There are only one or two more questions to ask. Did you have reason to dislike Señor Picare?'

'No.'

'You were not jealous of his lifestyle?'

'Did his money make me feel small? No. Did his potential destruction of marriages make me feel the moral duty to get rid of him? Like any sensible person, I leave others to fight their own battles.'

'His friendship with Señora Dunkling did not distress her husband and you?'

'Giselle didn't like him any more than I did.'

'Do you think she would agree with that? You are aware she often visited Vista Bonita on her own?'

'And know why.'

The door opened, Giselle entered. 'Are you finished?'

'I am,' Turner replied.

'Then we'd better move.'

'Señora,' Alvarez said, 'I should like another word with you.'

'We're already late for meeting our friends.'

'I will not delay you for very long.' Alvarez turned. 'Señor, if you would like to leave us.'

'I'm staying. You're not going to have the chance to bully Giselle.'

'I must repeat what I said earlier? I am reluctant to ask the señora to come with me to the post.'

'In England, the police would never act like this.'

'They would not offer the choice?'

'You know what I mean.'

'Don't make a scene,' she pleaded. 'If I think I'm in any danger, I'll shout loud and long.'

'If you . . .' Turner did not finish, left.

'Señora,' Alvarez said, 'you may wish to tell the señor I questioned you about Frank. If it becomes necessary, I will confirm that.'

'Why should I bother?'

'You might find it preferable to explaining the true reason – that on several occasions you visited Señor Picare on your own when it was not to treat him.'

'Do I look stupid?'

'I will ask Señor Turner to return and hear my further questions so that he can corroborate your answers.'

'He won't believe what you're trying to say.'

'That may be. Alternatively, he may recall times when you said you wanted a break, to be on your own; that you'd go for a long walk, drive into Palma and visit the shops.'

'What are you getting at?'

'I do not think I need to answer. Let me ask you again. Did you ever visit Vista Bonita unless it was to help the señor with his back problem?'

'What if I did?'

'I suggest that on those days, unknown to your husband or brother, your intention was not to treat Señor Picare's back.'

'That's a filthy suggestion.'

'Then you would call Rosalía and Carolina liars?'

'Who are they?'

'The cook and daily at Vista Bonita who notice the course of life there. Señora, did you have an affair with Señor Picare?'

'No.'

'You deny the possibility, aware of what that must mean to you if you are proved to have been lying?'

She stared at a wall, angry, undecided, then finally said with bitter anger, 'What if I did? Does that disturb your little suburban mind? Living with two men is shameful; as I'm sure you know by now, Turner isn't really my brother. And I suppose you think taking on a part-time third man is the work of a she-devil?'

'I should prefer to say, surprising.'

'You are not married?'

'That is so.'

'Then you've yet to learn that anyone in a closed relationship sooner or later learns life becomes stilted, boring; the excitement of pursuit or submission is replaced by the dullness of routine. Neil banished that dullness.'

Failing to appreciate the naivety of his words before he had spoken them, he said, 'But you were already living with two men.'

'And boredom is merely delayed, anticipation dimmed. Neil offered the revived pleasure of being pursued, the indulgence of delaying submission. Of course, in the end, even Neil became predictable. As has been said, pleasure cannot override repetition.'

'That may be true, señora, but few of us have the chance of learning whether it is true. Thank you for your help.'

'I cannot do anything more?'

'I think not.'

'You lead so peaceful and pleasurable a life?'

'I live very quietly with my cousin and her husband.'

'You share her?'

The thought of the nature of what Dolores's answer to that question would be, caused him to say loudly, 'Good God, no!'

'Bourgeois reticence?'

He sought an answer which would not make her laugh. 'If her husband learned what was going on, I would become homeless.'

'The next time they go on holiday, call on me to shed the dullness of your life.'

SIXTEEN

'I was propositioned again today,' Alvarez said.

Jaime lowered his glass. 'Was she tight or destitute?'

There was a call from Dolores in the kitchen. 'Who's destitute?'

'She'd hear a cicada shrill a kilometre away,' Jaime muttered.

'Was she someone we know?' she asked.

'Not unless . . .' Jaime fortunately realised for once that what he was about to say was highly inadvisable.

Dolores looked through the bead curtain. 'Was it?'

Alvarez hurried to prevent Jaime's replying. 'You've noticed the woman who begs near the Sa Nostra branch this side of the village?'

'I've never seen any beggar there and who would be so foolish as to beg near a bank where nothing is given away? Haven't the police tried to move her?'

'She has to be somewhere. She was married to a man who took off with another woman and all their money; she has to wear cast-off clothing and is desperately trying to find enough to rent an unreformed *caseta* before she's thrown out of where she is. I always give her something.'

'Why hasn't the husband been made to give her money?'

'She doesn't know where he's ended up. The woman was from Menorca, so maybe that's where the husband is now.'

'Then tell the policia in Menorca to find him.'

'They'll refuse since he's not committed any crime.'

'Being a man, you do not think it a crime to throw your wife away?'

'It's a civil, not a criminal, offence.'

'If the Minister of Justice was a woman, it would be a very serious crime. The Good Lord made a mistake when he introduced Adam.'

'If he hadn't, there would have been no Eve, no you, Jaime and me.'

'You have drunk so well, it was stupid of me to decide to cook one of your favourite dishes.'

'What is it?'

'*Granda de Patates*.' She withdrew.

'You like potato pudding?' Jaime asked with surprise.

'As much as a mash of chickpeas.'

'Then why's she think you do?'

'She doesn't.'

'She's right. You spent the morning in a bar.'

'She's probably cooking something we like, but said what she did because she wants me to understand I annoyed her.'

'You didn't say anything sharp.'

'Women seem to be able to guess when a man's lying.'

'You don't give that poor woman anything when you see her?'

'There is no poor woman whose husband has gone to Menorca. I made her up to explain why you mentioned a woman who was so hard up.'

'Why?'

'To provide a safety net. What if she also heard me tell you I had been propositioned?'

'She'd guess you'd struck lucky.'

'And if sometime in the future I turn up late for a meal, what's going to be her first thought? I'd taken advantage of what I'd been offered.'

'It was all a lie?' Jaime absentmindedly drank, emptied the glass, refilled it with Campo Neuvo. 'You made me believe all you said. So now I'm beginning to think you made up being propositioned just to annoy me.'

'You want me to ask in a loud voice what's annoyed you?'

'You can be a sod,' was Jaime's response.

'Is the superior chief there? Alvarez asked.

'Why should he not be here?' Ángela Torres replied.

'It is Sunday, señorita,' Alvarez replied.

'Were it my place to comment, I should remark that our work does not cease at a weekend even if there are those who believe it does.'

He leaned back in the chair, lifted his feet up on to the desk. The stress of overwork was one of the prime causes of strokes and heart troubles.

Salas spoke. 'What is it?'

'I have questioned—'

'You are who?'

The unanswerable question: whether or not to announce his identity to Salas when certain the impeccably efficient Ángela would have done so. It was a gamble which he constantly lost.

'Your silence names you Inspector Alvarez.'

'Señor, can silence name—'

'Make your report.'

'Following the unexplained death of Señor Picare, I have questioned Señora Dunkling and Señor Turner. The latter has provided the name and address of Frank Macrone who lives in—'

'Would it trouble you to inform me why he is presumably of some relevance to the case?'

'I have previously explained that, señor.'

'And that prevents your doing so now in order to bring him into focus?'

Every time a loser. 'Señor Turner is a friend of Señor Dunkling and he is of the opinion that Frank Macrone disliked Señor Picare because there was reason to believe Picare had been over-friendly with his wife.'

'Your task is to eliminate suspects, not enlarge their number. And do not strain your imagination by trying to explain why you have not yet questioned him.'

'I spoke to Señora Dunkling and learned that even though she is a happy member of the ménage à trois—'

'To use the word "happy" in such context is to deny the meaning of the word.'

'Although she had two partners, she also had an affair with Picare, which raises the question, would they have been angered by her unfaithfulness.'

'You can consider such a term in the circumstances? Llueso has become a modern Sodom and Gomorrah.'

'I wouldn't say it was that bad.'

'You recognise no limits?'

'I suppose one could say the local English have become unusually imaginative.'

'Were you to speak with honesty, I fear you would find reason to erase "unusually".'

'Frank Macrone's wife—'

'Her Christian name?'

'As I have not yet had the chance to speak to her or her husband—'

'Chance or energy?'

'Señor, it has taken a great deal of time to uncover the facts in this case.'

'You can now be certain Picare was murdered and name the murderer or prove beyond reasonable doubt that he drowned accidentally?'

'I'm afraid not.'

'Then you do not know the facts of the case, only some which are connected with it.'

'That's rather a fine distinction.'

'Which will escape you. As also, no doubt, has the fact that this is the fourteenth day of your investigation.'

'I have been too busy to count the days.'

'We may well disagree on the meaning of "busy". Do you understand that the purpose of your investigation should be to prove whether or not death was accidental; failing certainty, to learn whether one or more persons had motive for killing Picare, to judge if such motive was sufficiently strong to raise the presumption that the person concerned was probably the murderer.'

'Yes, señor.'

'Had your investigation been successfully conducted, you would have quickly identified all persons who might possess such motive, questioned them, and now would present me with the name of the probable murderer or, lacking any such names, the probability that such lack raises the probability of suicide. Instead of which, you name another suspect whom you have not questioned.'

'I wished to report to you, señor, before I spoke to Señora Macrone.'

'An excuse which thunders with the ring of familiarity. You will question her today.'

'It is Sunday.'

'For you, that is reason for doing nothing?'

'It is a day of rest for most people and they will be on the beach or spending time away from home. I am unlikely to be able to make any worthwhile progress until tomorrow.'

'You will discover if your hopeful optimism is justified after you have visited her home and failed to find her there. In addition, you will determine whether Russell did lie or Marta was mistaken.'

'As you wish, señor.'

'As I order.'

The bungalow, a kilometre from Cala Roig, was the last of three around the base of land which rose to fifty metres in a cone shape. The garden was not large, but the ground was newly worked, many roses were in flower, the low surrounding hedge was newly clipped. It always puzzled Alvarez that there were people who would undertake work which could never be completed. The door was opened by a middle-aged man, dressed in T-shirt and over-long shorts.

'Señor Macrone?' Alvarez asked.

'Yes?'

He introduced himself. 'I'm sorry to trouble you on a Sunday, but it is necessary.'

There was a call. 'Who is it Frank?'

'Be with you in a minute, Lee. Inspector, please come on in.'

The hall/entrada was lightly furnished. On the small table and by the side of the telephone was a cut-glass bowl in which were several different coloured roses, artistically arranged; on the tiled floor was an oval carpet, elsewhere an evergreen pot plant with a bark-like stem and many curving fronds and a small bookcase filled with paperbacks.

The door to the room on the right opened and a woman, younger than her husband, dressed with a touch of flamboyancy, stepped out. She stared with curiosity at the visitor.

'Inspector Alvarez, Leila,' Macrone said.

'Is something wrong?'

'He thinks maybe you helped yourself to that pearl necklace you so admired at the jewellers.'

'Do keep your schoolboy humour in check.' She turned to face Alvarez. 'Inspector, if Frank asks if the security van we sometimes see in the village outside a bank is worth attacking, don't humour, just ignore him. Do come on in.'

The sitting room was furnished in minimal style. The lack of physical comfort, as well as of visual pleasure, was emphasised when Alvarez sat on a chair which seemed to be all bumps.

'Señor, Señora,' he said, 'as you will probably know, I am concerned in trying to understand the unfortunate death of Señor Picare.'

His wife gave no indication she had listened. Macrone said, 'Then you're here now because you've been told he was after my wife?'

'Frank!' she said sharply.

'You think he won't have heard the latest gossip and is now wondering which version could be true, which malicious?'

'Must you . . .?'

'Well?' Frank Macrone looked at his wife.

'Nothing.' She looked down at her feet, angry and flushed.

Alvarez brought to a stop what, he thought, might become a heated argument. 'Señor, did you ever speak to Señor Picare about the nature of his behaviour towards your wife?'

'I told him that if he went on pestering Leila, I would cut his pleasures short.'

'Do you think he took your threat seriously?'

Macrone was about to answer when Leila interrupted him. 'You need to understand what did happen, inspector, in case you wonder what's been going on. We'd met Neil at a friend's party and found it pleasant to be with him because he had a good sense of humour and both he and Frank had similar tastes when it came to music. Our friend had a machine playing all the time we were there and they both thought it wasn't music but a row.

'A month or two later, we had an invite from Neil a day before Frank heard his father was seriously ill which meant he had to return to England immediately. I was downbeat because I knew Frank was going to be very upset because he and his father had always got on well together and, mea culpa, I decided to go to Neil's party hoping it would lighten life. When there, I made excuses for Frank's absence and Neil was very sympathetic. The next day, he asked if I'd heard how my father-in-law was, invited me to a meal to take my mind off my troubles. I knew his reputation, but he had seemed genuinely sympathetic, so I accepted, ready to defend myself. I need not have bothered. He drove me back from the restaurant after a very good meal, saw me safely inside, left.

'He turned up again a couple of days later. I told him Frank's father was not responding to treatment, he suggested it would help me if I could take my mind off the troubles even for a short while and suggested a trip on his motor cruiser with a friend of his, a woman roughly of my age.

'The next morning, I drove down to the port, parked, and found his motor cruiser. He helped me board, called to someone ashore to cast off. I asked where his friend was. He told me she'd had to call off at the last moment. I said then I was sorry, but I was going to do the same. He tried to persuade me by saying he had a very special packed lunch and there was a bottle of Krug in the refrigerator. I made it clear I'd prefer to return ashore. When I stepped off the gangplank onto the quayside, I met a friend and the way she looked and spoke made me certain she believed I'd returned from a trip with Neil, not just aborted one. As soon as I returned home, I rang Frank to say what had happened.'

'Did you see Picare again?'

'No. And the more I held him at two arms' length, the more eager he became. He phoned, sent flowers, even wrote a letter to assure me he sought friendship, nothing more, and was distressed I should think otherwise.'

'Did you keep his letter, señora?'

'Tore it up. Why should I keep it?'

'It would have shown you were telling the truth,' Macrone pointed out.

She faced Alvarez. 'You can't accept my word? You're wondering if he would not have continued pestering me unless he thought that before long it would be worth his while?'

'Señora, having met and spoken to you, I do not need proof

that you have spoken the truth.' He asked Macrone, 'Señor, do you have any doubts about what the señora has told me?'

'Of course I bloody don't. But it's your job to disbelieve anything you're told unless or until it can be proved to be the truth.'

'To disbelieve only when there can be doubt and here there can be none. When your wife explained what had taken place, did you face Picare?'

'I drove to his place and told him that if he ever approached her again, I'd make certain he didn't trouble another woman.'

'You threatened to kill him?'

'To castrate him.'

Small wonder there had been a furious row.

SEVENTEEN

'What day is it today?' Salas asked.

Alvarez gazed down at his desk as he sought to find reason for the question.

'It is Monday.'

'Yes, señor'

'My intention for asking is to remind you what day yesterday was.'

Alvarez wondered which of their minds was adrift. 'Sunday, señor.'

'That still holds no relevance for you?'

'Not really.' What the hell are you on about? he wanted to ask.

'Did you interview Señor Macrone yesterday?'

'Yes, as ordered.'

'I have received no report regarding it. My secretary has earlier rung your office three times without having the opportunity to speak to you.'

'I wasn't here, señor . . .'

'That is known as emphasising the obvious. Would you explain why you were not in your office and do so without introducing someone whom you had to meet because you thought he had important information for you, but it turned out he had none.'

'I was just about to ring you when you rang me.'

'To provide an explanation for your silence which now deserts your memory? Your report.'

'Señora Macrone has spoken freely. Her husband had to return suddenly to England because of the illness of his father and as a result of this, she went on her own to one of Señor Picare's parties. She would never be called beautiful because not all her features are in harmony, but as is so often the case, her imperfections tend to be more attractive than—'

'At the best of times, your judgments are suspect; when

they concern the female race, they become solely a judgment
on yourself. You will ignore all matters that are not directly
relevant to the case.'

'Señor Picare met Señora Macrone and became interested
in her, particularly when her husband was forced to return to
England. Picare employed the usual seduction techniques –
sympathy, admiration, possibly even poetry – he then added
the advantages which wealth permits: meals at luxury restaurants, small, but not necessarily cheap gifts, projected voyages
on his privately owned motor cruiser. As you will know, when
one normally eats *sobrasada* on a slice of *barra* and occasionally drinks cava, *Truffles à la maréchale*, *Homard thermidor*,
Poivres à l'impératrice certain events become inevitable,
people become irresistible . . .'

'To a woman of honour, nothing offered by anyone other
than her husband is irresistible. That you should consider
otherwise is yet one more indication of the values you hold.'

The line became dead.

Alvarez replaced the receiver. The phone rang.

'Inspector Alvarez,' Ángela Torres said, 'I have been
instructed to say you are to give me the details of your interview with Señor and Señora Macrone.'

He provided a bowdlerised report.

'One moment.'

Several moments later, Salas said, 'Have you yet not learned
to question a witness efficiently and effectively?'

'Yes, señor . . . Rather, no.'

'You would like to provide a less ambiguous answer?'

'No, I have not learned yet because yes, I have.'

'You are mentally disturbed?'

'As you have pointed out in the past, señor, a double
negative—'

'Were I granted the ability to retrace time, I would not take
the risk of explaining a double negative to you and would
forbid you, as I do now, to mention one. Your report is
incomplete.'

'I don't think it is, señor.'

'You told Señorita Torres that because Macrone's wife was
being pestered, he threatened Picare if this did not cease. You

omitted to describe the nature of the threat. This should have been detailed.'

'Señor, you asked Señorita to hear my report.'

'Who naturally noticed the error.'

'I decided that when truth can offend virtue, silence is golden.'

'Truth is virtue, virtue cannot be offended by silence.'

'Señorita Torres might have found the words used by Señor Macrone to be offensive.'

'You have forgotten what he said?'

'Macrone told Picare that if he bothered his wife one more time, he'd rip off his cojones.'

'You understand the consequences?'

'Picare might become a counter tenor.'

'The kind of remark to be expected from you. Macrone becomes the second man whom we have reason to name a suspect because of his delivered intention to punish his wife's adulterer.'

'Would-be adulterer, señor. There is no doubt that Leila Macrone utterly rejected Picare's advances.'

'You have reason for such certainty?'

'Having spoken to both her husband and her, there does not seem to be any need for proof.'

'Once more, you force me to ask myself if you possess the ability required by your job. You clearly have failed to question Macrone as if he was a suspect, you have not demanded to know where he was when Picare drowned, questioned others if they saw him that morning, asked those who live by the Puig what they noted during the morning. Perhaps you have at least ascertained the make, model and colour of Macrone's car or cars?'

'No, señor.'

'That is something I should expect you to have done.'

'If I thought Macrone was a man who had the character to carry out his threat, I would have done.'

'You saw no reason to override your thoughts? You overlooked Picare's legacy of ten thousand pounds, wealth to a man who is penniless?'

'On Marta's evidence, Picare was alive when Russell left Vista Bonita.'

'The value of her evidence was proved negligible by the cook and—'

'Rosalía.'

'You wish me to note you can recall her name? Did you not judge her evidence as by far the more trustworthy?'

'But taking everything into account, the fact is that Señor Russell is not well built or strong; I find it difficult to think he could seize Picare by the legs and drag him under the water with the necessary speed and force. Again, to commit a planned murder, one needs a strong, if perverted, character. Russell's character is just weak.'

'You have the knowledge and experience to judge character?'

'Sometimes, señor.'

'But perhaps this is not such a time. From the manner of your report, I judge you have not questioned him again, as ordered.'

'I have been concentrating on matters connected with Señor and Señora Macrone. I cannot do two jobs at once.'

'And frequently find it difficult to do one. You will ask Rosalía to confirm her evidence. You will learn the make, model, and colour of Russell's car. You will question others living in the same urbanizacion as Russell and learn whether anyone saw his car on the afternoon of Picare's death.'

'Witnesses can very seldom accurately pinpoint time, señor, and since they will have often seen his car, are likely to confuse such sightings.'

'Do you wish to conceive further reasons for not being able to carry out the investigation efficiently?'

'I question whether the likelihood of gaining relevant evidence from such a course would be worth the time involved.'

'A decision for me to take, not you.'

'I still don't think the motive for murder, if there was one, was money.'

'You wish to name an alternative?'

'Sex. It is difficult to explain why I should think that—'

'There is no difficulty in understanding the reason.'

'Picare's marriage was unhappy. Possibly the señora is frigid, far more likely it was the obvious pleasure he gained from naming his quarry and pursuing her to a successful conclusion.'

'There seem to be no limits to the unwelcome absurdities of which your mind is capable. You will do as I have ordered.'

Alvarez replaced the receiver. Having to talk to Salas induced thirst. He opened the bottom drawer of the desk and brought out a bottle of Soberano. It was empty. He had intended to replace it on his way to the office. Age was nibbling his memory.

Did he leave the office for his merienda? Salas might ring back with further demands and moans. Yet that was a danger which possessed its own safety net. If he was not in the office, it was because the moment he had finished speaking to Salas, he had hurried away to do as ordered.

He walked to Club Llueso and the welcome coolness of the air-conditioned bar. 'What'll it be? Fanta Orange?' Roca asked.

'Coñac, large, served in silence.'

'It's that kind of a day?'

'I've a boss who thinks I should work twenty-five hours a day.'

'Hasn't he learned one is your limit?'

'Do I have to go to another bar to be served a drink?'

'If you're not worried about getting only what you pay for.'

Alvarez braked to a halt, used a handkerchief to mop the sweat of fear from his face and neck. Whilst he'd been driving up the hill and when almost up to the house, a large bird had soared so close to the car, he had instinctively looked at it – a black vulture. Because of his brief inattention, the front off-side wheel had been only a few millimetres from the edge of the road. He'd turned the steering wheel with panicky speed to bring the car back to safety as his altophobiac fear had visualised the wheel going over, the car teetering, the loss of balance, the bone-rushing crash, the skin-stripping blaze . . .

'Are you all right?'

The nightmare faded. Rosalía was standing by the car which was motionless, on all four wheels, facing the front door of Vista Bonita.

She opened the driving door. 'What's the matter?'

He was unprepared to admit to his fears.

'Are you ill?'

'Just thinking.'

'From the look on your face, you shouldn't have been.'

He climbed out of the car. 'Thanks for worrying about me.'

'I wasn't certain it was you to begin with.'

'I've come to speak to you about something that's worrying me.'

'You still haven't understood the answer remains negative?'

'You're always ready to think the worst.'

'When you look hungry, it's not food you're after.'

'I'm not here for my pleasure.'

'Then at least on that score you won't be disappointed.'

'Let's go inside.'

'Why?'

'It's too hot in the sun to do what I have to outside.'

'Or inside.'

'You misunderstand me yet again.'

'Your misfortune is that I never do. If there's no reason for you to be here, you can clear off.'

'I've been ordered to speak to you and Marta.'

'What about?

'Señor Picare.'

'I've told you all I know and Marta's not here.'

'Is she ill?'

'Too troubled to come to work.'

'Then we'll go inside. And it's merely to have a word.'

She went indoors and he followed her into the staff sitting room. She moved a chair well away from any others, sat. 'I've work to do so hurry it up.'

'Tell me about the marriage.'

'Whose?'

'The Picares.'

'It was like any other. They'd become bored with each other and bickered.'

'Did the bickering ever end up in a real row?'

'Sometimes.'

'How serious?'

'They never came to blows, but there was the one time when I thought it would.'

'What was that row about?'

'How could I tell when it was in English?'

'You might not have understood, but gained an impression. Could it have been over his women?'

'Names were shouted, so it could have been.'

'What were the names?

'You think I took enough notice to remember?'

'The row must have upset him. Perhaps he looked to you for reassurance?'

'He'd no reason to think I'd offer any. In any case, my sense of charity became frozen the first time I went out with a man.'

'A gentle fire could melt it.'

'Not when lit with shop-soiled matches.'

'Tell me how the señora is.'

'As to be expected.'

'Is she well enough for me to speak to her?'

'You want to make her feel better by telling her that her husband was maybe murdered?'

'I'll keep things calm.'

'You'll keep out of her way.'

'I need to learn whether she knows anything which can help me determine if her husband died accidentally or was murdered.'

'You've as much emotional understanding as a dead frog. You are not going to worry her.'

'I've been ordered to.'

'By whom?'

'My superior chief.'

'Tell him I'm in charge of who does or doesn't see the señora and if he wants to argue that, he can come here and do so with me.'

'I'm tempted to pass on your message to learn the result . . . I suppose it'll be better if I leave talking to the señora until tomorrow.'

'Until I say you can.'

EIGHTEEN

Alvarez braked to a halt, climbed out of the car, walked towards the front door of Ca Na Porta. The door was opened by Eva Amengual 'What do you want this time?' she demanded as she watched a humming-bird hawk-moth busy itself around the flowers of a lantana bush.

'Rosalía told me Marta is not at work today.'

'What's that to do with you?'

'Is she well enough to have a brief word with me?'

'It is her mind which remains ill and talking to you will hardly provide a cure. My cousin is going to take her to Marineland to try to cheer her up.'

'She still believes she bears responsibility for the señor's death?'

'She imagines more than, I pray, happened.' Eva's hostility lessened. 'Inspector, would Señor Picare have divorced the señora and married my daughter?'

'No.'

'His lies were to encourage her to . . . to permit . . .?'

'Yes.'

'His death was just.'

'Perhaps, but wrong according to the law.'

'Does the law care how much a mother suffers when her only daughter is endangered?'

'The law serves legal, not human justice. Where is your husband?'

'Working the land. Where else?'

'Whereabouts?'

She directed him along an earth and small stone path which ended at a three hectare field bordered by a small orange grove. Forty years before it would have been usual to see men, women, and older children planting, watering, weeding, harvesting an assortment of crops ranging from potatoes to melons; now, even the men were unwilling to work so hard for so little, a

fact marked by the many small fields which were down to
grass or even untended and growing only weeds.

Amengual stood by a large estanque, ready to direct the
water into another rough irrigation channel. Alvarez walked
up to him; he was disinterested. Alvarez looked out at the
nearby rows of tomatoes, their side shoots untrimmed as was
the custom, with the result that each plant resembled a small
bush. 'You've a fine crop there.'

'You here to tell me what I know?'

Some would have been annoyed by the curt and aggressive
dismissal of praise; Alvarez was not. A true Mallorquin
accepted praise without hypocritically denying its validity. 'I'd
like a word.'

Amengual stopped the flood of water, used his mattock to
seal the water-filled channel with earth, unlocked the next one
by withdrawing a plug of earth. The released water began to
fill it. He rested the mattock on the ground, put a hand round
on to the small of his back.

The easing of back pain reminded Alvarez of the times
when, young, he had had to work on the land until he thought
he would never be able stand upright again. 'Like I said, I
want to talk.'

'I ain't the time.'

'I'll give you a hand after.'

'And have you muck everything up, like a pig among melons?'

'I did this kind of work when I was a kid.'

'That was long enough ago for you to have forgotten. You
want to talk about that shit-bag again?' Amengual stopped the
flow of water, walked across the land and sat in the shade of
an orange tree; Alvarez settled by his side.

They were silent until Amengual said, 'Swallowed your
tongue?'

'I've learned Marta's still very upset over Picare's death.
When he was alive and upsetting her, like any father, you must
have wanted to clear him off the scene.'

Amengual brought a pack of Ducados from his pocket, did
not offer it, tapped out a cigarette, lit it. Custom dictated that
to smoke or drink and ignore one's fellow was insulting. Alvarez
brought out a pack of Pall Mall, making it obvious he would

be smoking a better quality cigarette to that which he should have been offered. They smoked.

'You must have wanted to get rid of Picare,' Alvarez remarked.

'Weren't necessary since he did for that himself.'

'Did you pull him under the water and were maybe annoyed when he died immediately instead of taking his time and suffering?'

'I've a mind to throw you off my land.'

'Unwise. I'd know it was you who assaulted me and so you'd be in trouble. Pull Picare under in his own pool when no one's around and you reckon you'll never be identified. Where were you when he died?'

'How am I supposed to know when he died?'

'The second of May at around four thirty in the afternoon.'

'I was working the land.'

'How can you be certain of that?'

'Because I work it every bloody day from dawn to dusk if I'm to get enough money.'

'Wouldn't have missed much time or money when you drove up to Vista Bonita, pulled him under the water, returned.'

'I went by helicopter?'

'Suppose I tell you someone saw you up there on the day and not long before he drowned?'

'You can tell him he's a bleeding liar.'

'Why would anyone bother to lie about it?'

'Ask him and I ain't wasting any more time so you can bugger off.'

'I've more to talk about.'

'You'll be the only one listening.' Amengual used his shoe to force his cigarette stub into the soil.

'Where's Marta?'

'Don't matter since you ain't worrying her.'

'By answering a question or two, she may be able to convince me that you didn't murder Picare.' Alvarez waited for self-interest to overcome angry resentment.

Amengual stood, Alvarez did the same. They walked around the edge of the land and down to the house. Amengual opened the front door and shouted, 'Eva.'

She came through the entrada and was about to speak when she noticed Alvarez and remained silent.

'Wants to speak to Marta.' Amengual contemptuously indicated Alvarez with a thumb.

'Why?'

'Where is she?'

'In her room.'

'Get her down. I'll have a drink and him . . .' Another jerk of the thumb. 'He'll likely want one if it don't cost him.'

The main room, enlarged during the reformation of the building, had a sloping roof; the underneath of the tiles had recently been repainted with yeso which helped to lighten the room which had only a single, small window because of the problem of breaking into a rock wall. The walls were bare and the rocks, chipped into the required rough shape by hand, fitted into the stone jigsaw with a skill which had not been lost despite the few times it was required in modern houses. The fireplace was large, the furniture, plain, the tiled floor uncarpeted.

Eva went upstairs, Amengual into the kitchen. Alvarez looked at a large, framed photograph of a group of men and women in traditional dress, laughing and enjoying themselves. A photograph taken relatively recently at a social meeting, nostalgically reflecting the old times when costumes were traditional. Forgotten in the laughs were the facts that then there was little money and happiness had to be in the soul, not the pocket.

Amengual returned, handed over a glass three-quarters filled. The wine was primitive. Parker points would have hovered around zero, the wine declared undrinkable, yet for Alvarez it was a welcome gift from the earth, sun, and rain. Eva returned, accompanied by Marta, sad, defeated, uneasy.

'He wants to know something,' Amengual said, as Marta sat. 'Tell him.'

Alvarez greeted her and, since it was time for a lie, added, 'You're looking better.'

She murmured something.

'Thank you for talking to me. I've only one or two things to bother you about.'

She remained silent.

'I think you told me that Señor Picare and his wife seemed to get on quite well together?'

She nodded.

'Yet like other married couples, they did sometimes bicker?'

She looked at her mother.

'Tell the inspector, love. It doesn't mean they were always having rows. You've told us, you heard 'em arguing.'

'Just sometimes,'

Alvarez said, 'You want to say very little, or even nothing, because you would feel you were breaking their trust in you. But the truth is as important to them as anyone else. When they bickered, did it seem to you they were becoming angry?'

'No.'

'You never thought an argument might turn into a destructive row?'

She shook her head.

'The señor didn't shout at the señora and call her unfortunate names? She did not respond equally violently? I know you wouldn't understand their English, but one can usually judge from tone when someone's really angry and starts swearing. Did you ever think that happened or even that relations became so strained, violence was likely?'

She shook her head.

'Then I've nothing more to ask. Thank you for being very helpful.'

After Marta had returned upstairs and he had driven halfway to the post, he decided to change his destination to Vista Bonita in order to question Rosalía about the difference between her testimony and Marta's. Salas might ask him if he had done so and condemn him if he had not.

Rosalía's greeting was short and sharp. 'Here again? Why?'

'For the pleasure of seeing you.'

'A reciprocal pleasure I am denied.'

'Sorry to learn that. I think your dress is very attractive.'

'Have some of the buttons become undone?'

'I should like a word.'

'A one-sided pleasure.'

'How's the señora?'

'Fortunate, since she's on her own.'

'Is she better?'

'A couple of days are sufficient to overcome the death of a husband?'

'That depends.'

'On how self-interested one is.'

'On what I've been told. Look, it's better if we can't be overheard, so shall we go into the staff room?'

She hesitated, turned, walked across the entrada and into the small sitting room. He followed. Easy chairs were grouped in front of the large TV. She moved one well clear of the others, sat. 'Hurry it up.'

'What's the rush?'

'Something more important than talking to you.'

'But surely not as much pleasure. What do you have to do?'

'Cook a meal for the señora which is tasty enough to encourage her to eat.'

'Sausages and mash?'

'Chicken breasts with soft cheese, bacon and a light garlic sauce.'

'Didn't you tell me she hated garlic?'

'If she asks, I tell her I've used onions.'

'She doesn't suspect?'

'No.'

'The dish sounds like it could be really tasty. I'd like to try it.'

'Don't bother to wait for the crumbs.'

'What's its name?'

'There isn't one. It's my own recipe.'

'You've plenty of tricks up your . . . sleeve.'

'You're like a ten year-old who's just been told females are different.'

'I'm twenty and still learning.'

'And never will if you can't understand you'll never see forty again.'

'I've several years to go before I reach that benchmark. Do you remember I asked you how the Picare's marriage ran.'

'Did you?'

'I've been told they had arguments – what else is marriage

– but these were always mild. The señor didn't shout at the señora, never physically threatened her. That's a different picture from the one you gave me.'

'Have you been talking to Marta?'

'Why ask?'

'You seek the chance to meet a girl who's still young enough to ignore the fact that your breath has lost the scent of lavender.'

'I talked to her solely because I believed she could offer some valid information. I asked her about the state of the Picare's marriage. She described how they sometimes argued but was quite definite that there were never any serious rows.'

'Do I have to sort it out for you? She's not stupid even if it seems she must be, considering what went on between her and the señor. She knows people will be laughing at her for ever thinking of marrying a man old enough to be her grandfather.'

'It's become fashionable.'

'Among the smart set, but not on this island where women still know pride.'

'If she'd worried about other people's opinions, she'd have cut the relationship.'

'And lose her chance of never again being a servant? But he died and so, being a loser, she faces contempt, not jealousy.'

'I don't understand what she could gain by lying about the relationship between the señor and señora.'

'If it was accepted he had been behaving as if the marriage was as good as over, there would be a divorce, he would be free to marry Marta. People would be sorry for her because of what she so nearly had, but lost.'

'Complicated.'

'You need me to explain more simply? Tell me why else she should have lied to you.'

'Or was it you who got the relationship wrong?'

'As far as I'm concerned, it didn't matter if they were all love and kisses or had flaming rows, just so long as I was paid on time.'

'Perhaps you sometimes overheard them and got the wrong end of the stick.'

'And no doubt you also wonder if the señor and I studied

the Kama Sutra together and please can you find out how well.
You can't begin to afford the entrance fees.'

'Experience is more valuable than money.'

'Not when it's unwelcome.'

He drove back to the office and throughout the journey
bemoaned his inability to match her derogatory observations
until after any comment from him had become valueless.

NINETEEN

Alvarez dialled Palma. Ángela said to wait. As the seconds turned into minutes, his mind wandered along paths more pleasant than those of work. He was suddenly brought back to reality.

'Yes?' Salas demanded.

'Señor, I have spoken to—'

'You are?'

It was a childish game for a superior chief to play, but seniority allowed seniors to play it.

'Inspector Alvarez.'

'Have I not previously, indeed several times, pointed out the advantage of knowing to whom one is speaking?'

'But I told Señorita Torres who I was.'

'Who you are.'

'I have spoken to Marta and she told me Picare would argue with his wife, but never angrily. Rosalía, however, said they quite often disagreed furiously and, at least on one occasion, so violently that Rosalía expected him to hit his wife.'

'Did he?'

'Rosalía could not say. As you will understand it is very necessary to know who's accurately remembering what happened. I asked Rosalía if she could be wrong, Her reply was the question, why should she lie when she could gain nothing from doing so. She guessed I'd been speaking to Marta and remarked that Marta's mind was still very confused and it was unwise to accept without question what she said. Further, Marta might knowingly want to escape the truth.'

'Why?'

'If she had reason to judge Picare was a man with a violent character as well as a womaniser, she would be viewed with greater contempt if she believed he would have offered her marriage and she would have accepted.'

'Then her mind is less confused than you have been suggesting.'

'Why do you think that, señor?'

'It is not obvious that someone who can judge such possibilities is not mentally confused? And not long ago did you not assure me her evidence concerning Russell when by the pool was to be accepted?'

'Yes, but—'

'Yet you now judge that the worth of her evidence is doubtful.'

'I don't think that's quite how things are because—'

'Was Rosalía over-friendly with Picare? In the immoral times in which we unfortunately live, it should have occurred to you that she might have encouraged him.'

'I doubt it.'

'He appears to have committed adultery and immorality with Jovian enthusiasm.'

'Only when the señora was in England, not when she was here. Then, he had to watch his step. If she'd caught him at it, I guess she'd have given him hell for enjoying something she didn't.'

'A typical, unfortunate, immoral conjecture. Have you questioned Rosalía over her relationship with Picare?'

'I have not thought that necessary.'

'Why not?'

'A woman does not wish to be questioned over such matters; especially when she holds him in contempt.'

'You are unaware a puta always views her clients with contempt?'

'I have not the experience to judge.'

'You suggest I have?'

'Certainly not in a practical sense, señor.'

'You will question her.'

'Again?'

'You wish to contest my order?'

'Certainly not, señor.'

'You will speak to Señor Russell again.'

'For any specific reason?'

'You do not find it reasonable to ask him to repeat some of

his evidence in order to find out if he has changed it? Further, I will presume, not wishing to strain your imagination, that you have not yet questioned Macrone or those who live near Vista Bonita.

'Are you aware that despite the time which has elapsed, you are no nearer to identifying a motive for Picare's death?'

'That's true, señor. But that provides an advance in the problem of solving the nature of his death. Lacking a motive, it was an accident.'

'You are intent on turning a negative into a positive? A conclusion reached because it is desired and is very likely to be wrong.'

'Señor Russell?' said the receptionist at Hotel Tamit. 'Are you the policia who's been here before, asking about him?'

'I am an inspector in the cuerpo.' He hoped she would regret the solecistic manner of her mistake.

She had a sharply featured face and an inquisitive manner. He was not surprised when she further remarked, falsely casual, 'There's a problem?'

'We're trying to help him.'

It was obvious she would have preferred a crime of some monstrosity. 'Have you seen him in the past couple of hours?' he persisted.

'He went out to the beach after his coffee in the smoke room.'

Alvarez left, waited for a couple of cars, which had ignored the no entry sign, to pass, crossed the road to the beach. A brief search found Russell, lying on a towel, face up. He raised himself to a sitting position. 'An unexpected visitor. More questions?'

'Queries.'

Russell stood, pulled on a T-shirt, picked up the towel, shook and folded it. 'Where do you want to ask them?'

'Your room in the hotel.'

They crossed the road, entered the hotel, went up in the lift and along the passage to Russell's room. He used the phone to order a coñac with ice and a lager. He sat on the bed, Alvarez on a chair. 'What are the queries?'

'Did you come to the island to ask Señor Picare for money?'

'I've answered that more than once.'

'Why did you go to Vista Bonita that day?'

'What does that matter?'

'Do I have to remind you that you were there on the day Señor Picare died and had been in his company? Indeed, Rosalía was upstairs, in a room which overlooks the pool and heard the señor arguing furiously with you, because you asked for money.'

'Yet again, I did not.'

'Then where did the money come from with which you entertain young ladies?'

'I brought enough out with me.'

'You are forced to stay in this hotel, yet could afford to entertain? Why are you lying?'

'I'm not.'

'Your lying makes me wonder why. Did you murder Señor Picare in order to gain the legacy?'

'That's ridiculous!' he shouted.

'A reasonable probability.'

There was a knock on the door which was opened by a maid who carried a tray. She noted Russell's distressed state and that his shirt was in some disarray, looked briefly at Alvarez, hurriedly put the tray down on the small bedside table and left.

Alvarez stood, handed Russell the lager, picked up the brandy and sat once more.

'I . . .' Russell stopped.

'You realise that at this stage, the only sensible thing is for you to tell the truth?'

'Because of what had happened . . .'

'Yes?'

'It doesn't matter.'

'For you, it might well matter a great deal. On the day the señor drowned and not long before we judge that happened, Rosalía was upstairs in Vista Bonita. The windows were wide open and the room she was in overlooks the pool. She heard you and the señor having what she describes as a very rough row.'

Russell stared through the window.

'There has to be cause for anger. Whatever that was, it seems likely to provide the motive for Señor Picare's murder.'

'You . . . you're trying to say I killed him.'

'You had a meal with him on your first night on the island. Because you were in a hurry to see him?'

'You don't understand.'

'And won't until I hear the truth.'

'I did go there to ask him if he could lend me some money.'

'Lend?'

The suggestive question was ignored. 'When I went there, I met Marta after the meal. She was wearing an attractive brooch and I told her how well it suited her. She blushed, murmured the señor had given it to her, fled.

'That made me remember something Neil had said several years before at the pub when he'd drunk too well. If you've got money, you choose your target and she comes running. Cecily was behind the bar and told him that if he was a millionaire – it was before he sold the land – he'd have to look far and wide to find any woman who'd take a step in his direction. He replied that if he were rich, she'd visit his farm whenever she was invited.'

'Which, I gather, is roughly what happened. How does that have anything to do with your meeting Marta?'

'There was something else he used to say. If you take them to posh restaurants, drive them around in a sharp car, take them to theatres and they still hold out, give them some jewellery that looks expensive and you won't have to open the bedroom door, they'll do it for you.

'When I saw the jewellery on Marta, heard he'd given it to her, I realised he was after her and being young and unworldly, she couldn't judge why he'd been generous.'

'Why couldn't it have been a good-natured gift?'

'When a middle-aged employer gives a piece of jewellery to a young female employee?'

'You would not accept the possibility Señor Picare was aware of Marta's insecurity and thought the gift might provide her with the confidence she could gain from possessing something others didn't?'

'No.'

'Did you speak to Marta?'

'Warn her what he was after? To her, I was all but a stranger and she had no reason to believe what I said. She would have been embarrassed and shocked because I could imagine she would ever give way to Neil.'

'You did nothing.'

It had been as statement, not a question. Russell's voice rose. 'I was going to sit around after what happened to June?'

'Who is she?'

'My daughter.'

'You are married?'

'On paper.'

'Your wife stayed in England when you came here?'

'She'd already left me and taken June with her when she went to live with another man. I came out here to get over things. A few months after I arrived, I had a letter which had gone all around the Balearics because it had the wrong post code. She wrote that Peter, her new man, was trying to mess with June and would I have them back.'

Alvarez noticed Russell's fingers were tightly clenched. 'Did you not reply?'

'You think me such a shit, I ignored what she'd told me? She'd given me a telephone number. When I rang, a man told me my wife and June had left there and he couldn't say where they'd gone.'

'Have you heard from your wife again?'

'No,' he said, his voice low. He spoke more strongly. 'She had the name of this hotel so if I was here, she could write or phone me. For June's sake, I wanted to beg them to return. She had emptied our joint savings accounts and Mr Universe had great muscles, but nothing more. That's why, even knowing how much Neil would enjoy being lord of the manor, contemptuously handing a groat to a peasant, I asked him to lend me some money. I had to, for June's sake. I imagined Peter putting his hands on June, telling her it would make her feel happy . . .' He stopped abruptly, lowered his head.

'Sorry,' he mumbled.

Alvarez pressed the service button by the side of the bed.

The maid who entered, stared at them, her expression enigmatic.

'My friend,' Alvarez said, 'has just had some bad news and needs a drink. Will you bring the same as before – one coñac with ice, one lager?'

She left.

'I have to ask you something more,' Alvarez said.

Russell did not respond.

'When by the pool at Vista Bonita, did you accuse Picare of grooming Marta?'

Russell replaced the handkerchief in his pocket. 'Yes.'

'Did you threaten him?'

'I said I'd make him suffer if he ever touched her.'

'How did he react?'

'Laughed.'

'What did you mean by "suffer"?'

'I . . . I was so distressed . . .'

'In such an emotional state, it's probable you said you'd kill him since that was shortly before he died.'

'When I left, he was alive. I was so choked thinking about June, I went to a bar and drank myself stupid.'

'Which bar?'

'I can't remember.'

'Where is it?'

'I didn't kill him.'

'Where is the bar?'

'Somewhere in the port.'

'Because of the circumstances, you have to remember the name if you're to convince me you're telling the truth.'

Russell stood, went over to the window, stared out. It was a couple of minutes before he said, 'It seemed Italian . . .'

Alvarez waited.

'Bar Venezia.'

There was a knock on the door, the maid returned and placed two glasses on the bedside table, picked up the old ones. 'Who's paying?'

'I am,' Alvarez replied.

'Four euros.'

'It's Gran Duque dé Alba?'

'Aren't you used to paying for services?' She waited for the money, left after a hard look at Russell.

Bar Venezia was on the front, towards the western end of the port. It was always advantageous when wishing to question the owner of a bar to ask for a drink and pay for it. When Alvarez had finished a generous coñac, he said, 'I need to know if anything unusual happened here a few weeks ago.'

'Why?'

'Nothing you need worry about.'

'I worry about everything, especially the illegal, immoral increase in rates when the banks have made such a mess of things, people can't drink as they used to.'

'Is there somewhere at the back where we can have a chat?'

The assistant was told to carry on, the owner, followed by Alvarez, went into a small office, its space made much smaller by table, computer, filing cabinets and several unopened cases of San Miguel. There was only one chair. The bar owner, after muttering Alvarez might as well sit on it, settled on the edge of the desk.

'What is it you're after?' he asked.

'To know if you can remember one of your customers. He's English and was so concerned about something which had happened, he came in here and drank heavily one night a couple of weeks ago.'

'It used to happen whenever a busload of tourists turned up.'

'Late thirties, well-built, speaks a kind of broken Spanish. And while you're remembering, I'll have another coñac and maybe you'd like something?'

'You buying?'

'Yes.'

'Just joined the cuerpo?'

The bar owner shouted out the order. He said more quietly, 'There was an Englishman who came in here and drank like alcohol was about to be made illegal. Can't exactly remember what he looked like.'

'Was he plastered in the end?'

'Set in cement.'

'What happened?'

'We got him out before he collapsed.'

'Threw him out?'

'Called a taxi. Driver wasn't keen, but he made the Englishman pay up double what the fare was going to be before they started.'

'The Englishman was able to tell the driver where to go?'

'In the end. And if I'd been him, I'd of used the money he spent on booze to move to a better hotel.'

'D'you remember the name?'

'Hotel Tamit.'

Traffico, after the traditional complaints, provided the number, make and colour of Frank Macrone's car.

Alvarez left the post and walked along the shadowed side of the road, yet still felt as if every last drop of sweat was being wrung out of his body. His car did not have air-conditioning and the drive was equally debilitating. Since dehydration could be fatal, he stopped briefly at Bar Llueso.

Alvarez pressed the bell at the side of the front door of the bungalow below Vista Bonita. A woman, heavily made-up, opened the door. He introduced himself, began to explain who he was and why he was there.

She interrupted him. 'You don't look like a detective,' she observed, her words thickly spoken.

'I apologise,' he said facetiously.

'You're here because of them up top?' A nod of the head indicated Vista Bonita.

'Yes.'

'Best come in.'

The entrada was over-furnished . He followed her into the sitting room, equally overburdened, cooled by air-conditioning.

'I was about to drink,' she said. 'What would you like?'

'About' was obviously a mistiming. 'A coñac with ice, please.'

He watched her cross to a table at the side of one of the armchairs, pick up a glass, realise it wasn't empty and drink was left in it. She left the room, walking with care. He was

not, he accepted, going to learn anything from her, but at least she understood Spanish hospitality.

On her return, she handed him one glass then, to his surprise, sat at his side on the settee. 'What d'you want to know?' she asked.

'I'd like a word with your husband as well as you, señora.'

'He's doing what he always bloody well does, playing golf.'

The coñac was of some quality, yet he couldn't immediately name it. 'Señora . . .'

'Poppy.'

'Tell me what you can remember about the morning of Thursday, the twelfth of July.'

'Wouldn't remember, but it'd be as boring as every other day.'

'You can't say if you were here?'

'Where else? You think he'd leave me with the car when he needs it to go off and play golf?'

'Would you have stayed here all morning?'

'Must have done without the car.'

'Can you think of anything which might mark that day?'

'Like him spending the time with me?'

'Do many cars usually pass here to drive on up to Vista Bonita?'

'How would I know?'

If she often enjoyed as many drinks as she obviously had so far that day, she wouldn't. 'Might you have seen a brown Fiesta that Thursday?'

'What's that?'

'A car. One of the Ford models.'

'My father wouldn't have a Ford; it was common. You need to drink up so as you can have another.'

If other occupants of the houses and bungalows were as mind-away as she, it was going to be a waste of time to question them.

She stood, had hurriedly to put a hand on his shoulder to regain her balance. She picked up her glass with some difficulty, left.

Her husband was ill-advised to leave her on her own. As the Mallorquin saying put it: A woman ignored was easily persuaded. The blonde hair was almost certainly naturally coloured, her lips were shaped to be of use, her body delightfully proportioned, her short skirt, when drawn up as she sat, had revealed a generous proportion of attractive legs.

She returned, sat more closely to him than before. 'I only ever drink when someone else is here. I do it to be hospitable.'

As he only drank to be hospitable. 'Have you roughly any idea when your husband will return?'

'When it's too dark to see the ball.' She leaned against him. 'Do you play golf?'

'I'm afraid not. I lead a very quiet life.'

She edged closer; he felt the swell of her breast on his forearm.

'When you do play, what d'you like doing?' He didn't answer. 'You don't want to tell me because I'd be shocked? I wouldn't, no matter what you told me. There's no need to worry, Frank won't be back for a long time.'

It was dangerous to rely on one person's assurance as to what another would or would not do. He stood, she lurched sideways across the settee. Her skirt had risen higher, but she made no move to lower it.

'Thank you for the drink, señora.'

'Let's be more comfortable and have the next one in the bedroom.'

He crossed to the entrada.

'Are you one of them?' she shouted angrily.

He left, walked to the next-door bungalow. A dog barked, but no one opened the door in answer to his knock. There was small point in wasting more of his time.

He drove down to the port and parked off-road by the middle of the bay. The beauty of the scene – deep-blue water, almost enclosed by mountains whose rugged slopes were sprinkled with shadows due to outcrops of rock, criss-crossed with the many colours of sails, soothed his mind and enabled him to accept that nothing was more futile than to regret refusing what had been offered.

*   *   *

'I want to speak to the superior chief,' Alvarez said.

'You would like to speak to him,' Ángela Torres sweetly corrected.

He waited.

'Yes?' was Salas' greeting.

'Inspector Alvarez reporting on his investigation into the unsolved death of Neil Picare, señor.'

'Your flippant manner is unwelcome.'

He would always be in the wrong. 'Following your orders, señor, I have spoken to those living in the properties at the foot of Vista Bonita.' Since he had not specified 'all', he had not specifically lied. 'Unfortunately, I have not been able to learn anything of consequence and as I remarked previously, because the amount of traffic up and down the road is considerable, it is bound to be very difficult to find anyone to provide that. One lady had to ask me what was a Fiesta. Another husband was playing golf and the wife had taken the opportunity to drink rather more than was reasonable, so she was not a reliable witness.'

'Perhaps you were not a reliable questioner?'

'Why would you say that, señor?'

'You clearly did not question any of them as soon as you were ordered to do so.'

'I deemed initially I should speak to Russell.'

'As I ordered.'

'I learned the cause of the row which Rosalía overheard. Russell has a daughter, June. The marriage was not a success and his wife and June left him, despite the close and happy relationship between him and his daughter. When his wife wrote him a letter, he learned her boyfriend was trying to mess around with June. He immediately wanted to get in touch with her and persuade them to return. She'd provided a telephone number, but the letter took so long to reach him that when he rang, it turned out she and June had left there without providing any forwarding information.

'One day when at Vista Bonita, Marta proudly showed Russell a brooch which Picare had given her. He'd heard that Picare gave jewellery to any woman he was after and that made him certain he was after Marta. Russell went up to

Vista Bonita, found Picare in the pool, threatened what would happen if Picare continued to try to bribe Marta into willing submission.'

'He threatened to kill Picare?'

'He did not detail his threat.'

'We will accept that is what it was.'

'Señor, if you believe that here is the motive for which we've been searching and which would identify the man who dragged Picare under the water—'

'You challenge the obvious?'

'Initially, I viewed the information as you do. But then I learned he'd left Vista Bonita so mentally disturbed, he went to a bar where he drank himself silly. I made further enquiries and can confirm he was incapable of returning to drown Picare.'

'He is the last named suspect. Presume his innocence and we have to accept Picare died accidentally, perhaps due to entering the water with his head at the wrong angle and with too great a force. My instinct is, that cannot be right.'

'You have frequently told me, señor, that instinct is not to be trusted.'

'Its value, or lack of same, depends on the person concerned. You have failed to identify any meaningful discrepancy or contradiction in a suspect's evidence and will, therefore, question each one again, searching for what you may have previously negligently overlooked.'

'But—'

'You have your orders.'

'I've had a tempest of a day,' Jaime said, as Alvarez sat at the table.

'A mere zephyr compared to mine.'

'Do this, do that, why have you, why haven't you. Been on my feet the whole time.'

There was a call from the kitchen. 'Your zephyrs and tempests are but breezes for someone who has to run a house and is on her feet all morning, afternoon and evening. But being a woman, of course, she does not complain.'

'Just moans,' Jaime said, in a low voice.

Alvarez refilled his glass. 'I was propositioned again.'

'If I believed you, I'd want to know why in the hell you're complaining.'

'You think I'm lying?'

'Suffering from wishful imagination.'

'She didn't sit hard alongside me on the settee and ask what I'd most like to enjoy; suggest we went into a bedroom to be more comfortable?'

'You think I'm going to believe that?'

'Don't give a damn whether you do or don't.'

Jaime betrayed his disbelief was false. 'Why the hell does it always happen to you and never to me?'

'I'm good looking.'

'You'd make Dracula look friendly.' Jaime picked up his glass and emptied it. 'Admit you make it up to annoy me.'

There was a rustle from the string beads as Dolores put her head through. 'What's Enrique done to annoy you?'

Alvarez hurriedly responded to prevent Jaime's answering. 'I was telling him about a man I know who's won over a million on the lottery. It's always annoying to be told about other people's good fortunes.'

'For either of you to win a quarter of a million would be a catastrophe since you'd be dead within six months from a pickled liver.' She withdrew her head and, for a few seconds, the strings of beads knocked against each other.

Jaime drained his glass, checked Dolores had not reappeared, refilled it. 'Why tell her I didn't like hearing about other people's good luck? She'll hold that's selfish thinking and likely now won't concentrate on the cooking as she should. You've put her in one of her moods. Next thing, she'll be telling me we all get what we deserve. If that were true, I'd get five times the salary I do.'

'Is the table laid?' she called out.

'Women should do women's jobs, not expect men to do them.' Jaime straightened the tablecloth.

Alvarez drove slowly. His thoughts were resentful. He was to ask the occupants of all the houses below Vista Bonita – never mind if he had already questioned the occupants of any of them – and ask if he or she remembered seeing a brown Ford

Fiesta during a named interval of time on the twelfth of July.
If Salas possessed the normal appreciation of what was reasonable and what was not, he would have accepted that the odds
of gaining any worthwhile information were so low, the task
was not viable.

He slowed as he approached the first bungalow, regretfully
accepted that only a fool would take the risk, stopped outside
the second property, an undistinguished looking house.

A Señor Cartwright answered the front door bell, listened
to Alvarez's introduction of himself, suggested they went into
the sitting room.

'You want to know that?' he asked, surprise raising his tone.

'Naturally, I realise the practical difficulties.'

'Frankly, and no offence intended, I'd call them impossibil-
ities. I mean, there aren't that many cars that go up or down
which might seem to make it easier, but trying to remember
a brown Fiesta some good time afterwards, when I normally
don't take any notice of who goes by – there's no reason since
I doubt we and the deceased have any friends in common –
makes it, like I said, really impossible.'

Alvarez agreed. The problem was going to be how to explain
to Salas why he did not bother to question those in the other
homes.

TWENTY

Alvarez drove to Ca'n Porta. As he climbed out of the car, Eva Amengual opened the front door, watched him approach. He wished her good morning.

'How's Marta now?' he asked.

'Learning to live again.'

He gave the traditional response to that traditional remark. 'May she learn well and quickly. Is your husband here?'

'You think him a tourist with nothing to do?'

'He's in the fields? I'll find him and have a word.'

'What about?'

'I have to ask him more questions.'

'You told him you were certain he had dragged that piece of shit under the water. You want to insult me as well by saying I once worked in a house with green shutters?'

'I could never suggest anything so monstrously impossible. I accused him of nothing, just asked him if he had been in the pool with Picare.'

'Only someone like you could think that possible.'

'I am now certain he had no part in Picare's death.'

'Anyone but you would have known that from the beginning.'

'I need to find out if he knows something which he does not know he knows.'

'If there's someone who understands what you say, it's not me.'

'Whereabouts will I find him?'

'We have so many tens of hectares, I need to direct you to save you the trouble of looking. He'll likely be with the peppers.'

He walked along the rough path to the field in which Amengual was using a mattock to weed between rows. Amengual looked up. 'You again? Then you can do some work.' He indicated his mattock.

'Twenty euros an hour.'

'You ain't worth twenty cents.'

Alvarez brought a pack of Pall Mall from his pocket, tapped a couple of cigarettes free, offered them. 'Care to try one? I ask, because the last time I was here, you preferred to smoke your own on your own.'

Amengual hawked and spat. He withdrew a cigarette, put it in his mouth, lit a match for them both.

'I want another word,' Alvarez said.

'Ain't nothing more to say.'

'What you tell me may, as I mentioned to your wife earlier, give me the chance to find out that you know something useful you don't know you do.'

'She says she can't understand half of what you say because you talk so daft.'

'Shall we go to your place and get out of the sun?'

'There ain't no more wine.'

'Water will do.'

'You've been told you can drink it?' He walked to the end of the irrigated row of peppers, propped the handle of the mattock against the estanque, made his way to the house without bothering to check if Alvarez was following.

'He wants wine,' he shouted to his wife.

'From the look of him, he'll be dead when he don't.'

In the sitting room, she filled three glasses from the earthenware jug.

'Salud!' Alvarez drank, lowered his glass. 'It's nectar.'

'You saying it's the dregs?' she demanded pugnaciously.

'That it's good enough to serve to the gods.'

'As if you'd know what they like.'

Any hostility had disappeared by the time the jug had been refilled and partially emptied.

'I've a superior chief who's so suspicious of everyone, he often doubts himself,' Alvarez said. 'So when he heard you'd told Picare what you thought of him because of Marta, the superior chief got the crazy idea maybe you did the drowning. I'm here to learn something which will calm him down and make him accept that's nonsense.'

The Amenguals looked uncertainly at each other.

'Picare died on the twelfth of July, in the afternoon.'

They said nothing.

He addressed Amengual. 'Where would you have been then?'

'Where d'you think? Working in the field.'

'Did you see or speak to anyone who'd remember seeing you that afternoon? It was a Thursday.'

'Don't make no difference what day it was.'

She said loudly, 'You old fool!'

He looked at her, surprised and puzzled by her fierce intervention.

'You think you were on the land when they changed market day before the summer. You'd of been collecting me in the van.'

He spoke slowly. 'So I would. So I would.'

'You sell in the market?' Alvarez asked her,

'How else do we get a fair price?'

'Your husband collects you and the unsold produce in the afternoon?'

'There ain't nothing to bring back since there ain't no one else grows better fruit and vegetables.'

'You collected him from the market that Thursday?'

'Ain't I just said? Not missed a market in years.'

'Then your husband may have had reason to hate Picare, but he did not kill him.'

'Only the likes of you would believe he could.'

'Not seen you for some time,' said the barman in Bar Fernadol, on the western edge of Llueso.

'Been working too hard to have a moment's rest,' Alvarez replied.

'How's the work going?'

'Same as ever.'

The barman accepted his questions were not welcomed. 'What'll you have?'

'Orange juice.'

'What?'

'Comes from the fruit of an orange tree.'

The barman stared at him, said slowly, 'Now I've seen it snow in July!'

It was, for him, an unusual request, Alvarez accepted; it was probably the first time he had made it since a boy. But after all he had drunk with the Amenguals, he needed something neutral.

He carried the glass over to a table and sat. The Amenguals would be able to prove they were at the market on the time and date in question so there was no need to question them further.

Salas' orders had been explicit. Each of the possible suspects was to be questioned again. Was that a practical demand? Most would say it was reasonable to assume that when one half of a marriage learned the other half had been guilty of an affair, he or she would regard the intruder with angry hatred. Yet experience in life showed that the old-fashioned values of loyalty and morality had been tattered. Lynette Arcton had committed adultery, but her husband was dead, Leila Macrone denied adultery with Picare and evidence suggested her husband had believed her and ignored the rumour-mongers, so had had no reason to murder. Other relationships seemed equally devoid of a possible reason for individual retribution.

He picked up the glass and walked to the bar.

'Another orange juice?' the barman disbelievingly asked.

'A large coñac with ice.'

Half an hour later, refreshed, he drove along a minor road to the Palma/Playa Neuva autoroute and on to Llueso.

He awoke, stared up the ceiling and wondered if the rich enjoyed limitless siestas every afternoon. It helped to believe that if they did, they probably lost the pleasure of them. It must have been the devil who decreed that to enjoy too much of what one enjoyed would destroy the enjoyment.

Had Dolores considered him and bought a chocolate éclair from a pastelería? Whom did he question when he left home after coffee? Marta? Her mental stability was still a question mark.

Cecily Picare? It was reasonable to assume she must have known at least a little about her husband's amorous lifestyle, but could, or would not, furnish all the realistic details he needed to know. Señora Metcalfe? Did she only go to Vista

Bonita to learn tricks of cooking from Rosalía? Yes, if she was a good wife and considered her husband's pleasures; no if she put hers before his. Had Debra Crane seen Picare merely to remind him to pay his dues? Had Pierre Poperen discovered his wife's infidelities and avenged her dishonour? Russell claimed to have been concerned with Marta's welfare. He admitted pursuing one of Picare's women and might have infuriated Picare and caused him to refuse the money which would have enabled Russell to stay at the hotel, thereby denying him any chance of a reunion with his daughter. Giselle and George Dunkling enjoyed a ménage à trois which had been invaded by Picare; had his invasion caused one of the men to suffer murderous anger?

The possibilities had become too many, the task of gathering the evidence necessary to reject all but one, Herculean.

He would next question Madge Barrat, another of the neighbours living below Vista Bonita. With no apparent connection with Picare, aside from location, it need not be a prolonged and exhausting interview.

TWENTY-ONE

'The superior chief wants to speak to you,' Ángela Torres said.

'Perhaps wishes?' Alvarez suggested. 'When I said I wanted to speak to him, you corrected me.'

'When referring to a senior, a junior wishes, not wants.'

'With bowed head?'

There was a pause, during which he could hear voices, but not clearly enough to understand.

'Alvarez,' Salas said, 'Señorita Torres has referred to the unfortunate manner in which you have just spoken to her. You should not be surprised to learn that she found it objectionable.'

'I was only being very slightly sarcastic, señor.'

'As Pedro Antignac wrote, "Sarcasm is an ignorant man's wit". Why have I not received your report?'

'I gave it to you yesterday, señor.'

'And you have done nothing since then?'

'I questioned Amengual and Señora Barrat, but since I learned nothing of any consequence from either, I decided there was no reason to bother you with the results.'

'Your decision should have been to report to me immediately. You will now do so.'

'Amengual drives his wife to the local market where she sells the fruit and vegetables he produces. Because of the times at which he takes and collects her, he could not have been at Vista Bonita at the time of Picare's death.'

'Have you confirmed that the market was in operation on the twelfth?'

'It runs every Thursday throughout the year.'

'I repeat my question.'

Did Salas not understand that nothing prevented a market from operating on the specified day of the week?

'Have you confirmed he drove his wife there and brought her back?'

'They both confirmed that fact.'

'At what time did he fetch her?'

'At about four in the afternoon.'

'You have proof of that?'

He believed the Amenguals were telling the truth, so in a way it was fair to say their evidence was confirmed. 'Yes, señor.'

'Have you managed to do anything more?'

'I spoke to Señora Barrat and she—'

'Identify her.'

'She and her husband live in one of the properties below Vista Bonita. As instructed by you, I questioned the inhabitants of those homes and asked her if she had seen a brown Fiesta driving away on that afternoon since she might be able to confirm the time at which Russell had left there on the twelfth. Of course, to expect someone to note a car when that person has no reason to do so, not to mention the unlikelihood of accurately noting the time—'

'To anticipate failure is to fail. Have you determined how many brown Fiestas there are on the island?'

'I'm waiting for the information from the importers.'

'Until you receive this, do you not understand that little, if any, significance can be given to the sighting of such a car?'

'As it was you who ordered me to make the enquiries, señor . . .'

'Unfortunately, not in sufficiently simplified detail to enable you to understand what steps needed to be taken and the order in which to carry them out.'

'Judging by those whom I have spoken to, I don't think it can be regarded as feasible to continue to question other occupants in homes along that road.' Before Salas could comment, he added, 'However, as I said just now, I did speak to Madge. She and her husband live next to—'

'A surname?'

'Barrat.'

'What was her evidence?'

'She could tell me nothing that you would find useful and interesting, señor.'

In fact, it had seemed obvious that Madge had not been

involved with Picare, but it was easy to imagine he had met her and would have seen her as prey to be caught and tamed; perhaps her husband had returned unexpectedly or she had been guiltily unwilling to explain a lengthy absence from home.

'The result of your questioning is wholly negative?'

'As you have said, there are times when a negative can be as valid as a positive.'

'When considered intelligently. Have you spoken again to Marta to decide how much credence it is safe to give her evidence? Does the cook . . .?'

'Rosalía.'

'Yet again you consider you need to remind me?'

'I only mentioned her name because—'

'You will question the cook after speaking to Marta and will cross-check their evidence, with particular emphasis on the circumstances in which they heard Russell call out to Señor Picare when he was in the pool.'

'I will do so first thing in the morning.'

'This evening.'

'Señor, neither of them has a known motive . . .'

'Marta's father had a very strong one. Which is why you will ask her, without giving your reason, if at any time she heard her father vehemently condemn Picare and whether he was absent from home at the specific time.'

'I am morally reluctant to ask, without explaining why, a daughter to say something which might adversely affect her father.'

'I was not aware that morals have any part to play in your life.'

Alvarez parked, walked across to the front door of Vista Bonita, sounded the bell. As he waited, he gained pleasure from the view despite his resentment at being where he was in order to carry out orders with which he disagreed. He rang once more, was further ignored. He walked along one side of the house, checked the single side door was locked, rounded the corner and came in sight of the pool. Rosalía had been swimming and was standing by the steps at the shallow end. She was naked.

She saw him, climbed the steps, picked up a towel and began to dry herself.

His thoughts were a template for any man's mind in similar circumstances. He hurried forward.

'Am I embarrassing you?' she asked.

'On the contrary.'

'You don't mind seeing a woman naked?'

'Not when she's perfectly sculpted.'

'Then you approve of what you see?'

'Never more so.' His voice had thickened. He moved to her side.

'No closer or you'll get wet.'

'I'm waterproof.'

She spoke coquettishly. 'Remember, sweet inspector, I'm a good girl so it's see but don't touch.'

He reached out to put his arms around her, kissed her hungrily, cupped her left breast with his right hand, began to slide his left hand down her back.

'No!' She screamed. She struggled to free herself and when his grip did not loosen, clawed his face.

The sharp, unexpected attack caused him to release her. She ran into the house. He moved the tips of his fingers across his cheek, found they were bloodied.

For very many days, she had projected a sexy image, met sexual innuendo with sexual innuendo, inevitably led him to believe . . .

'You're bleeding.'

He had not heard Marta approach. His bewildered surprise was replaced by embarrassment.

'Didn't you know?' Marta asked.

He said nothing.

'I thought because you're a detective you must know about her and the señora.' Marta brought a handkerchief from a small pocket in the front of her frock, dabbed away the blood on his cheeks. 'You should see a doctor.'

Who would want to know the circumstances of his injury. 'It's nothing.'

'Take my hankie and hold it against your cheek.'

He wanted to explain, to try to excuse his behaviour, but

believed that to do so would exacerbate the contempt she must surely be experiencing. His bewildered embarrassment caused him to say, 'I'll return your handkerchief as soon as it's been cleaned.'

He refilled his glass with brandy from the bottle in the bottom drawer of the desk, regarded the telephone as if it was a spitting cobra.

He finally dialled.

'Senior Chief Salas' office,' Ángela Torres said primly and proudly.

'I want to speak to the señor.'

'You wish to do so. Wait.'

He drank. He'd been hoping Salas would not be there.

'Yes?'

'Señor, I have—'

'A name?'

'Inspector Alvarez.'

'Do you think that eventually you will be able to understand the need to introduce yourself? What is the object of this call?'

'To tell you, señor, that the motive for the murder of Picare was not money, as you suggested at the beginning of the investigation.'

'Your grounds for such conclusion?'

'Señora Picare and Rosalía enjoyed a relationship.'

Alvarez waited.

'That is all you have to say?' Salas demanded.

'I thought you weren't commenting because you were so surprised.'

'Since one of them is an employer and the other an employee, the relationship is one that is hardly a cause for surprise.'

'I'm not referring to such a relationship, señor.'

'Can there be any other?'

'For the señoras, it had become also a personal one.'

'I suggest you ring off and compose a legible report before you attempt to deliver it.'

Alvarez drank quickly. It was absurd he should need to explain certain facts of life to Salas whose prudery should have been banished by work long ago. That it had not could confirm certain rumours concerning Salas' marriage. 'Señor, the two were lesbian partners.'

Another silence. Then: 'Your authority for this statement?'

'The experience of someone.'

'Who?'

'I have promised never to reveal the name.'

'A promise you had no right to give since this is an ongoing investigation and the informer's evidence may well prove essential.'

'If I had refused to give my promise, I would not have learned the nature of the motive which finally confirms Señor Picare was murdered.'

'You should have succeeded in gaining the information by offering a retractable promise.'

'Understanding the relationship explains certain facts. When Picare died, his wife was naturally shocked, yet she suffered far more than one might expect when the marriage was far from a happy one. So why was this?'

'You can provide an answer which is not totally beyond belief?'

'She knew the nature of her relationship had somehow become known to her husband – hence the bitter rows between them. She had every reason to believe that as a consequence he would demand a divorce and her affair with Rosalía must be destroyed. It was Rosalía who decided there was one way in which to prevent this happening.

'When she learned I was investigating the death of Señor Picare, she was all playful and come-on. Yet as is now clear, the interest of any man was unwelcome to her.'

'A woman will hardly be described as playful with anyone other than a young child and I have no idea what is the meaning of "come on".'

'The manner in which a woman behaves when she wants to indicate she is interested and probably willing.'

'Your knowledge of matters in which a cultured mind has no interest never ceases to depress me.'

'She hoped her behaviour would avoid my becoming aware of her true feelings.'

'You say you learned the truth of the relationship from a

third person whom you promised not to identify. Since you must realise that his or her identity will be important in a trial, would I be wrong to consider it possible there is no such third person and he or she has been introduced in order to conceal you have been guilty of conducting the investigation in a manner which is prejudicial to the reputation of the cuerpo?'

'I have always been guided solely by that, señor.'

'For the sake of everyone, I will accept your reassurance.'

'Quite early in my enquiries, I leaned about a bitter row, almost violent, between the Picares, but at the time there was no reason to think this was caused by anything other than the señor's womanizing. Then when the relationship between the señora and Rosalía became known, I remembered those rows and how bitter they had become and judged Picare had learned about his wife and Rosalía. A man from an ordinary background made wealthy by luck is going to be very conscious of his image as seen by friends and acquaintances, in particular those from grander backgrounds than his. He would be convinced they would laugh at him if they learned his wife was a lesbian carrying on an affair with his servant. He will have told his wife she had to get rid of Rosalía or he would divorce her and make certain she got as little of his money as possible.

'The two women faced disaster. Cicely Picare was too old to return to a job in a bar, Rosalía with her cooking skills would find little difficultly in obtaining another job, but how likely was it that they would then be able to enjoy each other's company?

'Rosalía found the solution, but aware it would horrify Cicely, never discussed it. She subtly encouraged Picare, waited until Cecily was away for the day, suggested she and Picare had a swim together. To him, this would lead to a much desired conclusion. When it was too late, after she had lured him up to the deep end so that his head was just above water, she suddenly and violently, pulled him under.'

'It has taken you a very long time to uncover the truth,' Salas said.

'Because she used every possible means in which to cover her guilt. She mentioned the regular visits of women, named several without admitting that the visits of two were perfectly moral. When I asked her to help me in checking the ability when in the kitchen to hear someone by the pool, she spoke only in a whisper. When I went to the pool, she lied and told me she had heard nothing.'

'It has taken you a very long time to uncover the truth.'

'But for the information I received after I had agreed never to reveal the name of the provider, señor, it perhaps never would have become known.'

'Have you arrested Rosalía?'

'I judge that at the moment there is not sufficient proof to do so and unless she confesses, there is unlikely to be enough in the future.'

'You will question her again and obtain her confession. And in future, this will, hopefully, persuade you to accept my judgments. At the beginning of this investigation, I said that the motive for Picare's murder would prove to be money, not sex as you so wrongly maintained.'

'With respect, señor, it was sex that was the cause of the murder.'

'Initiated and inflamed by the greed for money.' Salas cut the connection.

In the sharp sunshine, Vista Bonita could appear to be a home of taste, wealth and gracious living.

Alvarez walked up to the front door, rang the bell. Marta opened the door. She seemed to be very nervous and chatted for a while before he asked, 'Is Rosalía here?'

'She . . . That is . . .'

'Tell me.'

'She . . . When I arrived, the house hadn't been unlocked. I have a key to the back door. I found nothing had been prepared for the señora's breakfast. Her bell kept ringing and I hurried up to her bedroom. She demanded to know why breakfast hadn't been brought up to her. Rosalía's missing. What am I to do? The poor señora is beside herself . . .'

Alvarez sat in his office, a well-filled glass on the desk. The airport had rung back to report that Señorita Rosalía Mulet had left Palma airport and flown to Paris before any request had been made to block her departure.

Salas would accuse him of incompetence. The moment he had learned of her disappearance, he should have reasoned she would try to flee Spain, unwilling to face the possibility there would be sufficient evidence to name her Picare's murderer. He should have made contact with every channel of departure from the island and ordered her to be detained. Salas would list a dozen more things any other inspector would have done.

He drank, lit a cigarette, considered matters. Should an inspector, appointed to serve the law, regarding its demands as sacrosanct, knowing it was all-embracing and designed to protect the many from the few, accept it was unable to prevent a man from using his wealth to persuade women to betray their marriages and the distress that his hunting must cause? Did justice not demand a man should be prevented from seeking fresh gratification from a young, naive teenager who was likely to become the first victim of many, since perversity fed on itself. Could justice be served by a crime?

Salas would be outraged by the questions. Better not to try to justify any of the events which had led to Rosalía's escape. A broad back was more worthwhile than an over-active conscience.

Alvarez drank deeply, refilled the glass.